PROJEKT 1065

ALSO BY ALAN GRATZ

Prisoner B-3087
Code of Honor
Samurai Shortstop
The Brooklyn Nine

PROJEKT 1065

ALAN GRATZ

SCHOLASTIC PRESS

NEW YORK

All rights reserved. Published by Scholastic Press, an imprint of Scholastic Inc.,
Publishers since 1920. SCHOLASTIC, SCHOLASTIC PRESS, and associated logos
are trademarks and/or registered trademarks of Scholastic Inc.

The publisher does not have any control over and does not assume any
responsibility for author or third-party websites or their content.

While inspired by real events and historical characters, this is a work of fiction
and does not claim to be historically accurate or portray factual events
or relationships. Please keep in mind that references to actual persons, living or
dead, business establishments, events, or locales may not be factually accurate,
but rather fictionalized by the author.

Library of Congress Cataloging-in-Publication Data available

ISBN 978-0-545-88016-9

10 9 8 7 6 5 4 3 2 1   16 17 18 19 20

Printed in the U.S.A. 23
First edition, October 2016
Book design by Nina Goffi

For Bobby
and
Brenda Gratz

DINNER WITH NAZIS

IT'S HARD TO SMILE WHEN YOU'RE HAVING DINNER with Nazis.

There were Nazis all up and down the long table, talking and laughing and eating. There were Nazi soldiers in their gray German army uniforms. There were SS officers, members of Adolf Hitler's private Protection Squadron, in their black uniforms and red armbands. There were regular civilian Nazis who didn't fight in the military, who ran banks and factories and newspapers and wore suits and ties and Nazi pins.

And then there was me, Michael O'Shaunessey, wearing my brown long-sleeved shirt, black shorts, white knee socks, and black hiking boots polished to a shine. And just like the SS, the most fearsome killers in all the land, I wore a red armband with a big black swastika in the center of it, the hooked-cross symbol the Nazis plastered all over everything. I wore the uniform of the Hitler Youth, Germany's version of the Boy Scouts. Because I was a Nazi too.

Or at least I was pretending to be.

"More cake?" the Nazi next to me asked, offering me another slice. Light from the chandelier glinted on the silver skull pin on his collar.

"Um, sure. Thanks," I said. "That's very kind of you." I remembered to smile, even though it took effort. I hated pretending to like these people, hated pretending to agree with their awful hatred of the Jews, hated pretending I wanted them to win the war and conquer the world. But I smiled because I had to. If they ever discovered I wasn't really one of them, my family and I would disappear into a concentration camp, never to be seen or heard from again.

"Your German is so good!" the woman on my other side told me. She was the wife of a captain in the German army. "If I didn't know your father was the Irish ambassador, I would think you grew up here in Berlin!"

I sagged in my chair. I heard this every time my family attended one of these dinners. I wasn't exactly the blue-eyed, blond-haired "Aryan ideal," but with my flawless German accent and my brown hair that fell like a mop into my brown eyes, I could pass for an average German boy any day. I wasn't proud of it, but it was definitely useful.

"Michael's always had a good head for languages," my father said in German. He sat across from me at the table, my mother two seats down from him. "We've only been here for six years, but he already speaks better German than I do!"

1937. That was the year my father was named Irish ambassador to Germany and we moved from London, where he'd been stationed, to Berlin. It was 1943 now, and I was thirteen years old. Things had changed so much in those six years. Berlin had been a wonderland when I first arrived, all towering columns with eagle statues on top and red flags fluttering from every building and parades ten thousand people strong. Hitler was already the chancellor of Germany, and the Nazis, his political party, were well in control. Germany wasn't at war yet, and not everybody was a Nazi back then, but it was hard to argue with their success. Everywhere I'd looked I'd seen faces full of smiles and laughter. But then, overnight, the party had ended. Not the Nazi Party. They had only gotten stronger. The other party — the feeling of unbounded German cheerfulness — was gone. I had finally seen the horror behind the smiles, and so had the rest of the world.

What happened that one night still haunted me.

"Michael's always had an exceptional memory, haven't you, son?" Ma said, breaking into my thoughts.

"It's true," my father said. "Michael reads in German, tells jokes in German. I think he even dreams in German!"

The adults around us at the table gave him a polite chuckle. Da the diplomat, doing what he did best. His mustache widened as he beamed at me, but the eyes that peered at me over his glasses weren't smiling. They were reminding *me* to smile. To be friendly. To play my part.

I picked up my glass of grape juice and took a drink to hide my frown.

"You are a better German than some Germans," the Nazi who

had offered me cake said. His name was Trumbauer, and his rank within the SS was Obersturmführer, which meant senior assault leader. He was a tall, thin man with slicked-back, jet-black hair, and a nose like a parrot's beak. "Just today, we raided the home of a German couple who were hiding a Jew in their attic. Right here in Berlin!" He shook his head as if he couldn't believe the stupidity of some people.

"How did you know they were hiding a Jew?" the woman next to me asked.

SS-Obersturmführer Trumbauer cut out a bite of cake with his fork and lifted it. "Their son reported them."

I shuddered. Their own son, ratting them out to the secret police. I couldn't imagine ever doing something like that to my own parents.

"What happened to them?" I asked.

"Hmm?" SS-Obersturmführer Trumbauer said, swallowing his cake. "Oh. The Germans were taken into protective custody at Dachau, of course. The Jew was shot while trying to escape."

The SS-Obersturmführer's words rattled me, and I knocked over my glass trying to set it back down. It struck the rim of my plate and shattered, sending glass and grape juice everywhere. I caught my reflection in every one of the tiny shards, half a dozen little Michael O'Shaunesseys looking up at me in horror. Suddenly, I was back again on that Berlin street, that night four years ago, when everything had changed.

When I'd finally learned what monsters the Nazis really were.

KRISTALLNACHT

IT WAS A COOL NIGHT IN EARLY NOVEMBER, 1938. I WAS eight years old, going on nine. My parents and I had just been to see a movie—a German film about the Olympics, which had been held in Berlin the year before we moved there. I was upset because I'd wanted to see *The Adventures of Robin Hood* instead. I'd read the book and wanted to see the American movie of it, but the Nazis had banned the film from Germany.

I hopped from the sidewalk into the street and back again, pretending to be Robin Hood fighting the Sheriff of Nottingham as we walked home to the Irish Embassy. I loved the idea of Robin Hood protecting the poor and the helpless from the evil King John, especially because John was the king of England. If I weren't Irish and already born to hate them, I had plenty of other good reasons for loathing the English.

Then we heard the first crash. The three of us froze. The crash was followed by a woman's scream, and the acrid smell of smoke bit at my nose as a black cloud rose over the rooftops the next street over.

"A fire!" Da said. "Hurry! We have to help!"

We ran for the street corner, but before we got there five men in brown shirts and red armbands came around the turn carrying axes and sledgehammers and paintbrushes and torches. One of them smashed a store window with his ax, and my father threw out an arm to hold me and Ma back. Glass showered the streets, shattering into a thousand bright shards. A man dipped his brush into a can of paint and then slathered it all up and down the front of the shop, painting something on the wood. Across the street, two more men broke the windows of a department store and tossed red paint all over the shoes on display. I didn't understand.

"Go. Move," Ma said, snapping us all out of our stupor. "We have to run."

"Why? What's happening?" I asked, but my parents were already dragging me away.

More shouts. More screams. Far off in the distance, a siren. We ran into a side street and stopped again. Shards of glass covered every inch of the street like ice, crunching under our feet. Every window had been shattered, and the word *JUDE*—the German word for "Jew"—had been painted on storefronts. Sometimes there were even little cartoon pictures of Jews. They had big noses and round heads and dull looks on their faces.

"My God, they're finally doing it," Da said. "They're going after the Jews."

I didn't understand what he meant, but I was afraid. Men wearing plain clothes and carrying axes had broken down the door of a synagogue, where Jewish people went to pray. The men began tossing prayer books and scrolls into the middle of the street. One of the men with a torch bent to set fire to the pile, and another man — a Jew, I guessed — came running out of an apartment building nearby, trying to stop him. The other men caught the Jew, and one of them struck him in the head with the wooden handle of his ax. The Jewish man dropped down to the street, the broken glass clattering beneath him, and the men gathered around him and beat him with the handles of their axes while their comrade set fire to the pile of Jewish relics. I gaped in horror, my heart thudding in my chest in time with the whacks of the ax handles, until my mother put her hand over my eyes and pulled me away.

"We have to get back to the embassy," Da said.

I pushed my mother's hand away and dragged the sleeve of my coat across my eyes. I hadn't even realized I was crying. "That man — they were hurting him. We have to go back and help him," I said.

"We can't, love," my mother whispered. She was crying too, I realized, and that scared me even more.

"Keep your heads down," Da told us. "Keep your heads down, and don't say anything or do anything."

Every street we turned down was strewn with broken glass and filled with men carrying sledgehammers and axes. It was happening all over the city. Some of the rioters wore the brown shirts of the SA, the Sturmabteilung, the thugs of the Nazi Party. But more of them wore ordinary woolen trousers and suspenders and white work shirts with the sleeves rolled up. Regular citizens who wanted to run the Jewish people out of town.

We were close to the embassy when we came upon a squad of Gestapo, Germany's secret police, loading men into a truck. At last, the police were rounding up the rioters! A Gestapo man stopped us and spoke to my father. I didn't know much German then, but I understood that he wanted to see our papers. He told us to stay where we were while he checked in with another officer.

"They're rounding up Jews," my father whispered. "Taking them to the labor camps."

I frowned at the men being loaded into the truck. Why were Jewish people being arrested? The Jews were the ones the Nazis were attacking! I wanted to shout at the police, tell them they were doing everything backward. To make them stop. But I was helpless. A little boy. I couldn't even speak their language.

My mother grabbed my father's arm. "Davin. There."

A man across the street was trying to sneak away in the shadows.

"*Ein Jude! Er versucht abzuhauen!*"

The cry had come from above me. I looked up and saw a boy about my age hanging out the window. The boy was yelling and pointing at the man across the street who was trying to get away. I knew enough German to have understood the word *Jew*. He was telling on him to the police!

One of the Gestapo men saw the Jewish man trying to escape. He called out for him to stop, but the man ran. The Gestapo man pulled out his gun and fired.

Bang! Bang! Bang!

The shots rang loud in the street, drowning out my cry of "*No!*" The Jewish man arched wildly as one of the bullets hit him, and he stumbled forward into one of the shattered storefronts, falling face-first at the feet of mannequins splashed red with paint. A sharp piece of broken glass poked up through the back of his shirt, stained red with his blood. He was dead.

"No!" I cried again, but my mother pulled my face to her coat to muffle my screams. I pushed and fought to get away, but she was too big, too strong. I didn't know what I was going to do if I got free. I just wanted to do *something*. Anything.

The Gestapo man with our papers walked back over to us, crushing shards of glass under the heel of his boot. I stopped struggling and held my breath. What if they took us away too? What if they shot my mother? My father?

The Gestapo man said something in German. He must have told us our papers were in order, because Da dragged us away. We held one another close, stepping over the glass. I kept my eyes on the ground, where I saw my reflection in each and every one of the shards of glass, hundreds of little Michael O'Shaunesseys looking back at me in despair.

"We have to do something," I whispered.

"We *are* doing something," Da told me.

"What? What are we doing?" I asked. "We're just running away."

Da and Ma exchanged a look.

"We have jobs, Michael. Roles to play here," Ma said. "Important ones. And if we fight these people right here and now, we can't do those jobs anymore."

"What, you mean being ambassadors? What good is that when people are dying?"

"We're not only ambassadors, Michael," Ma whispered. "We have another mission. A secret mission."

"*Megan,*" Da said warningly.

"If he's going to share in the danger, he should at least know the truth of it," Ma said.

Da sighed and gave in. And that's when they told me their secret. Our secret. Right there on a Berlin street, in the middle of what later came to be called Kristallnacht. The "Night of Broken Glass."

MY STRUGGLE

A DARK STAIN OF GRAPE JUICE UNDER MY BROKEN GLASS soaked into the tablecloth like blood, and I jumped up. The grape juice had spilled onto my lap while I'd been lost in my memory of Kristallnacht. Now it stained my Hitler Youth uniform.

"Oh, dear!" Ma said, standing up. "Is there someplace where Michael can get cleaned up?"

Servants were already descending on the table to mop up the spill. The lady of the house, a woman in a burgundy dress with a white pearl necklace and earrings, stood and gestured to one of the servants. "Of course. It's just around the corner and down the hall on the right. Greta will take you."

I hurried out of the dining room. "I can do it myself," I said. I definitely didn't want anyone to come with me.

I heard Ma apologizing for me. "I'm sorry. Now that he's thirteen, he won't let me do anything for him, either. He'll be all right."

I ran down the hall toward the bathroom, and then, with a quick look over my shoulder to make sure no one had followed me, I snuck up the stairs instead. SS-Obersturmführer Trumbauer's story about the boy turning in his parents really *had* rattled me, but I had always planned to have an "accident" with my grape juice. A little spill on my uniform was just the excuse I needed to disappear for a few minutes.

There was a long hallway at the top of the stairs stretching left and right. It was the biggest house I'd ever been in, but that made sense. The man who owned the house, who had invited my father, my mother, and me to dinner with a tableful of important Nazis, was a bigwig at Daimler-Benz, a German automobile company getting rich making engines for Nazi tanks and planes and submarines.

I didn't have much time. I hurried down one of the hallways, peeking in through the doors until I finally found one that looked like a study. The walls were lined with bookcases, some of which held trophies and pictures of race cars. I hurried to the big desk that backed up against a wall of curtained windows. It was night, and the room was dark, but I didn't want to turn on the overhead light and draw attention to myself. I clicked on the green glass desk lamp instead, recoiling in fear that even that amount of light was too much. But I had to be able to see to find what I was looking for.

People didn't just hand you their secrets. You had to go hunting for them.

I started with the papers on the desk. Internal company memos, official purchase orders from the German government, personal correspondence. All probably very interesting, but not what I wanted. I riffled through the desk drawers. There was a sound in the hall, like floorboards creaking under the weight of a person, and I froze. I reached out to the light, my hand hovering over the chain, but there wasn't another sound. I left the light on and scanned the desk, trying to think where it would be hidden. Not in plain sight. Not in an official letter.

There was a little toy car sitting on a leather-bound book, and I picked up the car to examine it. I poked at it, peered inside it, pulled at the wheels, but it was just a toy car. I set it aside and picked up the book. It was a copy of *Mein Kampf*—"My Struggle," the book Adolf Hitler wrote while he was sitting in a jail cell in Munich for trying to overthrow the government, back before I was born. Now that Hitler ran Germany, *Mein Kampf* was required reading for anybody in the Nazi Party. Or at least required *owning*. Despite a playing card tucked into it as a bookmark, it looked like the book had never been opened.

The playing card. I glanced at the page number to be able to put it back where it was, and looked at the card under the light. It was a jack of spades. I turned it over, then ran my fingers down the edge. Was it thicker than usual? I couldn't tell. I squinted at the edge under the light. Was there a seam there? I ran my fingernail down it, but it didn't separate. Maybe this wasn't it. Maybe I was wasting time. How long had I been away from the dinner party? Had they sent one of the servants to look for me?

My fingernail caught. There *was* a seam! I very carefully worked my fingernail along the edge, trying not to mar the card or tear it, until I got to the corner. I pinched both edges of the seam between my fingers and pulled, and the front and back of the card peeled apart. Inside, printed where no one could see it, was row after row of numbers. I peeled the card the rest of the way apart and read the numbers straight through one time, absorbing them.

The floor outside creaked again. I rolled the two halves of the card back together, stuck the card back into the book, and clicked off the light. The doorknob turned, and the door groaned on its hinges. Someone was coming into the room!

NOWHERE TO RUN

I STEPPED BEHIND THE CURTAINS ALONG THE BACK WALL, as the door opened. The curtains wavered from my movement, and I pinched a tiny part of them between my fingers to stop them from stirring. The floor creaked. Someone was in the room with me! I held my breath for the click of the light switch.

But it didn't come. I could hear the swish of clothes, the careful footfalls. But the person didn't turn on the light. Not the big overhead one. I heard the *chick-chick* of the desk lamp, and light glowed through the thin curtains in front of me. I could see the silhouette of a person through the curtain. Could they see me? Had I put everything back on the desk the same way I'd found it?

My stomach did somersaults, and suddenly I wished I hadn't had that extra piece of cake. The person in the room moved again, away from the desk. I heard the clink of glass, the brief, quiet slosh of liquid. *What was going on?* I had to know. I could see the dim figure of the person through the curtain, could tell he or she was bent over something, not looking in my direction. Slowly, carefully, I peeked out from behind the curtain . . .

A man in a dark suit stood over a little table on the other side of the room. He was a servant, I realized. The man who'd met us at the door. The butler. The table had glass bottles on it. Drinks. He was pouring a drink for someone. But who? Everyone else was downstairs, weren't they?

The butler glanced around to make sure no one was watching, and I ducked back behind the curtain. I saw his shadow raise the glass to his own lips and drink down whatever it was in one long gulp. He'd poured the drink for himself! I let out a silent breath of relief. All I had to do was wait for him to leave.

A light flashed behind me suddenly—the bright wash of a searchlight, the ones the Germans used to search the skies for Allied bombers. It startled me, and I turned to look out the window.

Which was a mistake.

The courtyard below was a straight shot down from the window. I closed my eyes, but it was too late. My head swam. My knees buckled. I had to grab for the latch on the window just to keep myself on my feet, and it rattled under my weight.

I was deathly afraid of heights.

"Who's there?" came the butler's startled voice.

The silhouette of the butler came closer. All he had to do was pull back the curtains and he would find me. I tried desperately to think of some excuse—I'd gotten lost on the way to the bathroom, I'd seen the race cars on the shelves and come in for a closer look — but none of them explained why I was hiding behind the curtains with the lights off. I was going to be caught, and my family and I would be thrown into a prison camp. There would be an international incident.

The butler's hand wrapped around the curtain. My heart thudded in my chest. I looked left. Looked right. Backed away as close as I could to the window.

I had nowhere to run.

THE MISSION

THE BUTLER'S HAND SLID AWAY FROM THE CURTAIN, AND he crumpled to the ground. Behind him stood another silhouette, shorter and rounder.

"Michael?" the shadow whispered. It was my mother! I stepped out from the curtains, my heart still racing, and almost tripped on the prone form of the butler on the floor. My mother was a small, dimple-cheeked woman with her brown hair cut short and curled, wearing a simple but elegant green dress. I was almost as tall as she was, and we were both definitely smaller than the butler.

"Did you — ?" I started to ask, but I could see the butler's chest rising and falling. He wasn't dead. Just asleep.

Ma held up her handkerchief. "Chloroform. I always keep a bottle in my handbag for emergencies. Did you get it?"

"I got it. But what about him?" I asked, nodding at the butler.

"What was he doing in here? Did he see you?"

"No. He came in and poured himself a drink."

Ma smiled. "Likes to have a nip of the good stuff, does he? Can't blame a soul for that. But I'm afraid he's going to get in trouble for it this time. Help me drag him to the chair."

Together we wrestled the butler into the reading chair beside the table, and Ma took a bottle from the table and poured some of it on his shirt before leaving the bottle in his hands.

"They'll think he had one too many, poor dear. But it's the only way to cover our tracks. Let's go."

Ma and I went back to the table, where everyone had moved on from dessert to cigarettes and coffee. All I wanted was to get out of the house before the butler upstairs was discovered. Before anyone could suspect that we'd had anything to do with it. But if we left right away, we would look even more suspicious. Ma gave Da a slight nod to let him know the business was done, and we settled in to listen to our host boasting about Germany's success in the war.

"Poland, France, Luxembourg, Denmark, the Netherlands, Belgium, they have all fallen in the great German avalanche that is sweeping Europe, and once the Sixth Army prevails in Stalingrad, Soviet Russia too will fall. And after Russia, we shall finally defeat the English!"

There were smiles all around, except from my family. My father cleared his throat and my mother looked at her plate.

"But not our friends in Ireland, of course, who have remained steadfastly neutral throughout the war," our host said magnanimously, raising a glass to my father. Da smiled politely and returned the toast.

We all knew that being neutral hadn't helped Denmark, Norway, Belgium, the Netherlands, *or* Luxembourg when the Nazis decided they wanted those countries. Germany had overrun them all shortly after invading Poland in 1939, just a year after Kristallnacht, setting off a world war.

Now, four years into the war, the Germans were after Russia and England, who were holding them off only with the help of the Americans. But Ireland had just won its independence from England before the war, and so we'd decided to sit this one out—which was why we still had an embassy in Berlin when hardly any other country did. But we were under no delusions. If Germany ever wanted Ireland, they would help themselves.

"I think it's time we were going," Da said, putting his napkin on the table. "We'll want to be getting home before the Allies start dropping their bombs on Berlin again."

That shut them up quick. It was a chilly reminder that not everything was coming up roses for Germany, and I loved my da all the more for saying it.

Everyone else stirred to leave.

"Send for the butler," the lady of the house told one of the servants.

Ma rose quickly. "We'll see ourselves out. Thank you for a lovely evening."

Soon we had made our escape and were in the car on the way back to the embassy.

"I assume you two had something to do with the missing butler?" Da asked as he drove.

"Michael ran into a spot of trouble," Ma said. "But it's nothing we couldn't straighten out."

Da thumped the steering wheel. "Damnation, Megan. I don't like using Michael in this business. It's dangerous! What if he'd been caught?"

"He wasn't," Ma said. "And even if they're suspicious, they won't find anything missing, will they, Michael?"

I shook my head. Ma gave me a pleased look and pulled a small notepad and pencil from her handbag. "Here. Not that you're likely to forget it, but write it out so we'll have it down."

I took the pencil and paper and copied out the long strings of numbers, exactly as I had seen them. I could remember them as though I was looking at a photograph in my own head. It was a trick I'd been able to do since before I could remember.

I handed the notebook back with the numbers written out. "What is it?" I asked.

"The location of a new engine factory," Ma said, tucking it away.

Da sighed. "I'll get them sent out in tomorrow's diplomatic pouch to Dublin."

I sat back in my seat, proud that I was doing something at last, something to fight back against the Nazis. Something to make up for that night four years ago when I'd felt so helpless, and for every night in between.

I had found the secret codes and memorized them. Ma had covered my tracks. Tonight she would decode them, and in the morning Da would send the coordinates back to Dublin using a secret code of his own. There, Irish Intelligence (even though they were supposed to be neutral) would secretly pass along the location to the British.

And a week from now, maybe two, Allied bombers would fly over that hidden German engine factory and bomb it back to the Stone Age.

This was the mission. This was the secret my parents had shared with me four years ago on Kristallnacht.

Ireland might have officially been neutral, but *un*officially, its ambassador to Germany and his family were spies for the Allies.

THE GERMAN LOOK

A LIGHT SNOW FELL ON THE SIDEWALKS OF BERLIN AS I walked to school the next morning. But at least snow was all that was falling. Half the buildings on the street were roofless, hollowed-out husks, victims of the relentless Allied bombings. Bombing Berlin was easy — it was the capital of Germany. Unlike the secret engine factory I'd discovered the location of, the Allies knew right where Berlin was. The British and the Americans took turns dropping bombs on the city — the British at night, the Americans during the day — sending us scrambling for the air raid shelters every few hours. But even after spending two hours in the middle of the night belowground, showered by grit from the concrete ceilings and feeling the dull thud of the explosions rattle their teeth, the people of Berlin were up and ready to face the day.

They emerged from their houses grim and determined. Or maybe grim and resigned. Some Germans must have gotten up every day and thought, *Hitler's right! We're the master race! Soon we'll rule the world!* But there had to be more people, lots more, who got up every day and thought, *If I just keep my head down and do what I'm supposed to do, maybe I'll make it through this in one piece.* There was nothing to do but go to work for Nazi Germany, for Hitler. To refuse meant arrest, and arrest meant the concentration camps. Everybody knew the concentration camps were awful places where awful things happened, but nobody ever talked about it. That way they could pretend it wasn't really happening.

People talked about plenty of other stuff they weren't supposed to, but only after a quick glance over their shoulder to make sure no one else was listening. Everybody did it so much there was even a special word for it: *Deutscherblick*. The "German Look." You did the German Look right before you said Germany might be losing the war, or complained about the food rations, or told a joke about Hitler. Because someone was always listening, always waiting to turn you in to the Nazi secret police. Always ready to rat you out to prove how loyal they were, even if they had said the very same thing yesterday.

The Berlin I walked through on the way to school was a quiet, suspicious city. People kept their eyes down, whispered if they had to talk, crossed the street to avoid having to give the Hitler salute to someone they knew in case they didn't say "Heil Hitler!" loud enough or raise their arm high enough. Nobody wanted to call attention to themselves. Nobody wanted to stand out. Nobody wanted the Nazis to notice them. Just walking to school was like trying to walk past a sleeping bear.

I had a test coming up that day, but I wasn't too worried about it. Nazi school was a joke. We spent most of the time doing physical education—playing games, running races, exercising. What little time we spent in the classroom was spent listening to the teacher tell us all about the glorious (and short) history of the Nazi Party, or teaching us how to tell German Aryans from "subhumans."

The history stuff I always aced. I have a good memory for things, like the secret numbers I'd read off the playing card. All I have to do is see or hear something one time, and it sticks in my head like a song you can't get rid of. It had helped me pick up the German language, and helped me memorize answers for tests, but it had made me a kind of freak too. And when you were an Irish kid at an English boarding school, like I was when my da was stationed in London, being a freak got you beat up. Daily.

Here in Berlin, it might get me killed.

HITLER YOUTH

IN SCHOOL, I HUNG MY COAT ON A PEG AND TOOK A SEAT
near the back of the room. I didn't have any friends at school on purpose, so I sat alone. My class was all thirteen-year-old boys. Forty
of us. No girls. They had school in an entirely different building.

None of the boys were studying for the math test we had today,
because none of them cared. Almost all of them, like me, were in
the Hitler Youth. We were all going to move from the Jungvolk—
the junior Hitler Youth ranks—to the senior Hitler Youth squads
in a year's time when we turned fourteen. At eighteen, we would
graduate from the Hitler Youth into the Reich's Land Service and
work for free on a farm in the country for a year, and after that,
we would join the army or the navy or the air force and fight in
the war. What did we need to worry about math for?

I tugged on the collar of my Hitler Youth uniform. I hated
the thing. I felt like a traitor wearing it. But if you were a boy in
Nazi Germany in 1943, you were in the Hitler Youth. It was
a requirement. Some of the boys in class were in my Hitler

Youth troop, but not all of them. The troops were arranged by neighborhood.

The only boys in the class who weren't in the Hitler Youth had been kicked out or weren't allowed in until their parents joined the Nazi Party, and they sat wary and miserable in the front rows, trying desperately to avoid the rest of the boys, who were allowed to bully them without punishment. If those poor boys didn't find a way to join the Hitler Youth before we graduated, they wouldn't have any kind of future in Nazi Germany. They would get drafted into the German army at the lowest ranks, and sent to Russia to die in the snow.

A boy stood by the desk next to me. I recognized him. His name was Fritz Brendler. He was new—he'd moved to Berlin only a few weeks ago. He was barely taller standing up than I was sitting down. The Hitler Youth uniform he wore was two sizes too big for him, and his legs and arms stuck out of it like the wooden stick limbs of a marionette. His nose was long and thin, his blond hair cut so close he was almost bald, and his ears, the only parts of him that were regular size, looked so huge on his little head that they stuck out like the wings on a bomber.

I could sense Fritz hoping I would turn and say hello, but I didn't. I didn't want a new friend. Definitely not a German one, who might be a rabid Nazi for all I knew. I had a job to do, and a German friend would just get in the way.

"Sit down, sit down, you little wretches," Herr Professor Doktor Major Melcher said, giving a tardy student a hard smack on the head with his ruler as the boy tried to slip by him into a desk. It was time for Nazi school.

HERR PROFESSOR DOKTOR MAJOR MELCHER

NOBODY LIKED HERR PROFESSOR DOKTOR MAJOR Melcher. For one thing, he had too many titles. The Germans loved their titles. Because he was a man you had to call him Herr, the German word for "mister." Because he was a teacher, you had to call him Professor. Because he had a doctorate from Heidelberg University, you had to call him Doktor. And because he'd been a major in the German army, you had to call him Major. Herr Professor Doktor Major Melcher. It took so long to ask him if you could go to the bathroom, you could wet yourself. We should have just been glad he didn't have two doctorates. Then we would have had to call him Herr Professor Doktor Doktor Major Melcher.

Herr Professor Doktor Major Melcher was old and wrinkly, with a bristly white mustache you could have used as a horse brush, and a liver spot the shape of Czechoslovakia on his forehead. He used to be a college professor until all the college-age students were sent off to war, and he was super mad about it and never let us forget it. The only reason anybody put up with him at all was because he'd fought in the First World War, and fighting was about all anybody in Germany respected anymore. I was surprised he wore a brown woolen suit and tie instead of his old uniform and pointy helmet.

Even though I wasn't his biggest fan, I had a soft spot for the old codger. I'd gotten the impression he didn't love the Nazis. It was nothing Melcher had said or done — anything that explicit would have gotten him hauled off to a concentration camp or reenlisted in the army, even though he was too old to fight again. It was just the way he talked so lovingly about the way things used to be. I felt he was a kindred spirit. A fellow faker.

"It's already enough that I waste my time on you ignoramuses when I should be teaching at university," Herr Professor Doktor Major Melcher told us. "Sit down and shut up, all of you. Before you take your math tests, I have two items you will no doubt consider to be good news. The first, as you may have heard, is that the Führer has announced that Berlin is now officially Jew-free."

There were smiles and clapping all around. I gave a fake little smile to mask my disapproval as Fritz, the new boy, turned to nod and grin at me. The Germans had been carting the Jews away to concentration camps all over Germany ever since the Night of Broken Glass, and now, according to Herr Maggot Hitler, they were gone from his capital city.

"The second," Herr Professor Doktor Major Melcher said, "is that the decision has been made to call up all seventeen-year-old Hitler Youth members directly into the German army."

The room erupted in excited conversation. Seventeen-year-olds fighting in the army? For the German government to call up senior Hitler Youth members to the army was one thing; to announce that they would be skipping the usual year of service working on farms in the countryside was even more extraordinary. That meant the Nazis were drafting boys just four years older than all of us straight to the front lines.

And I knew why. The rest of the boys in the class only got the news the German government gave them, but my family and I had a radio that could pick up the BBC News Service from London. The truth was, the German Sixth Army had just been forced to surrender to the Russians at Stalingrad after a six-month siege, a loss of more than 285,000 German soldiers. German radio was still listing the names of the tens of thousands of soldiers who'd died *before* the surrender. The Nazis were scrambling, trying to build their numbers back up after their disaster on the eastern front. The BBC News called it a turning point in the war, a shift in the favor of the English, American, and Russian Allies. For the first time in the war, the Nazis were on the ropes. I let myself smile about it while everyone else thought I was smiling about getting to fight for the Nazis sooner.

"As a result of the senior Hitler Youth members being called into active duty, the age for graduation from the Jungvolk to the Hitler Youth proper is now thirteen, not fourteen," Herr Professor Doktor Major Melcher told us, "which means all of you little brats are moving up into the regular Hitler Youth a year earlier than you thought. Next week, in fact."

NAZI MATH

THE CLASSROOM EXPLODED IN HAPPY CONVERSATION.

"Yes!" Fritz said, clenching his fist beside me. "This is great! Into the real Hitler Youth a year early!"

I was excited too. Entry into the senior Hitler Youth would mean even better chances to gather information for the Allies. Now, instead of having to wait to sneak into rooms during dinner parties, I would be given a position of real service in the city, where I could dig up some truly useful Nazi secrets. But then I remembered—to become a senior member of the Hitler Youth, you had to pass a series of physical tests, and there was one I knew I couldn't pass, and never would. I sank in my chair. Just when my career as a spy was about to take off, it was going to crash and burn.

"All right. Enough," Herr Professor Doktor Major Melcher said. "If this were a university classroom, we would already be studying calculus. The mathematics of the heavens. As it is, I must debase myself with the mathematics of firebombs and distances marched. Clear your desks for your test."

I shared Herr Professor Doktor Major Melcher's distaste for our math exams. Nazi math was always about war stuff. Questions like "A squadron of 346 bombers drops firebombs on an enemy city. Each airplane carries 500 bombs. How many fires will be caused if 30 percent of the bombs are hits and only 20 percent of the hits cause fires?" Or "The Jews are aliens in Germany. In 1933, there were 66,060,000 inhabitants in the German Reich, of whom 499,682 were Jews. What was the percentage of aliens?"

I sighed and attacked the test like the French Resistance attacking the occupying Nazi troops, but hoping for better results. When we finished, it was time for one of our many outdoor Hitler Youth training exercises. Officially, school and the Hitler Youth were separate, but whatever the Hitler Youth wanted—like time away from school to exercise and train—they got. Which in the dead of German winter was even more unbearable.

"If you're afraid of freezing to death, don't worry," Herr Professor Doktor Major Melcher said with barely hidden disgust. "I understand some of you will be keeping warm today by burning *books*."

DEGENERATE FILTH

A BONFIRE ALREADY BURNED IN THE MIDDLE OF THE street, built out of split timber and broken furniture from a house that had been bombed out by the Allies. It reminded me of the bonfire the men had built in the street during Kristallnacht, the orange flames just beginning to flicker in the broken glass at our feet as my parents and I turned the corner.

The heat coming off the bonfire here and now was inviting in the bitter February cold, but it was hard to enjoy it, knowing that soon we'd be heaping piles of books on top.

The Nazis used to have book burnings like this all the time. Back when Hitler first took over, he ordered that all the "un-German" books be pulled out of schools and libraries and burned. And the "un-German" books were pretty much *every* book. People were supposed to burn their own books too. The Nazis had huge book-burning ceremonies where they tossed all the offending books on the bonfire while they sang Nazi songs and celebrated being stupid.

By the time I moved to Berlin in 1937, they were pretty much done with book burnings—mostly because they had already burned every book in Germany. But every now and then, they discovered somebody's hidden stash of "degenerate" books, and they made a big show out of burning them in the street, as a lesson to everyone else.

We stood in a line in the street while our Hitler Youth leader marched up and down in front of us. His name was Horst, and he was fifteen. Horst was a thick-necked, donkey-faced idiot whose idea of a good time was throwing rocks at stray dogs.

"The era of Jewish 'intellectualism' is over," he told us, regurgitating lines the Hitler Youth organization had pounded into his thick skull. "The German man is not a man of books, but of character. Of action! These *books*," he said, squeezing one of the offending volumes in his fat hand as if it were a cat he was trying to strangle, "are evil spirits of the past. We consign them to the flames so the world will know there is no place for decadence and moral corruption in Germany!"

No, I thought. *No place for decadence or moral corruption. But room for book burnings and concentration camps.*

"From the flames of this degenerate filth," Horst said, flinging the book into the bonfire, "the phoenix of a new German spirit will rise in triumph! Now get inside there and cleanse that house of its corruption!"

This was why we were really here. Not to learn a lesson, but to do the work the SS didn't want to do. We broke formation and ran up the steps into the thin, gray little row house. Just inside, in a cold, lifeless parlor, stood a small pile of pathetic-looking books, like the last rotting apples left on the ground after a harvest. While the other boys fell on them, grabbing up handfuls to haul outside, I took in the room. There were a few pieces of furniture — worn-looking upholstered chairs, scuffed end tables, a once-red rug whose color had faded to a kind of rust brown. But everything personal was gone. There were no mementos on the fireplace mantel, no knickknacks on the tables. Bright round circles of color stood out on the pale wallpaper where pictures had once hung, and an empty vase in the corner sat on its side, knocked over. It was unbroken, but no one had set it to rights.

The cold settled on me, chilling me to the bone. This house was dead. And so too, probably, were the Germans who had lived in it. Who had they been? An old couple, living out their last years together? A young couple, making a new start with hand-me-down furniture? A family with children — perhaps a boy my own age?

Whoever they had been, they were as dead as this house. Or soon would be. Carted off to a prison camp to die, all for the sin of hiding forbidden books in their home.

I picked up what was left of the books and followed the other boys outside. They weren't thinking about who had lived there, or where they had gone. They were merrily tossing the books on the fire, happy for any chance to throw something and watch it burn.

I tossed one book onto the fire at a time, slowly, so Horst wouldn't see me standing around doing nothing. My skin crawled, as if I was consigning little bits of my soul to the fire with each book I threw in. But like smiling at a Nazi dinner party or memorizing facts about the Nazis for tests in school, it was all about the bigger mission. It was all part of the game. If it meant them letting me stick around to steal their secrets so the Allies could win the war, I'd burn every last book in Berlin.

"Hey! He doesn't want to burn the books!" one of the boys yelled, and I flinched.

I was busted.

THREE CHEESES TALL

I NEARLY JUMPED OUT OF MY SKIN, THINKING HE WAS
talking about me. That I'd been too slow to burn my books, that
I'd let my disgust show on my face. But the boy was pointing
at someone on the other side of the fire.

"The *Dreikäsehoch*," he said. "He's not burning his books."

Dreikäsehoch was one of those crazy German compound
words where they mash a bunch of little words together to make
one big mouthful of a word, the way *Obersturmführer* meant
"senior assault leader." *Dreikäsehoch* meant "three cheeses tall,"
like three wheels of cheese stacked one atop the other. It was a
silly way of saying somebody was short.

And the short kid, in this case, was Fritz Brendler. The new
kid. He was so small he looked like he was ten years old, not thirteen. He had four books in one arm, clutched to his chest, and
another in his hand. And he wasn't throwing any of them on
the fire.

Fritz stepped back, his eyes wide with fear, as Horst and the other boys surrounded him.

"What's this?" Horst demanded. "You don't want to burn these books?"

"I didn't — I just — " Fritz stammered.

Come on, kid. Don't do this, I thought. These boys were animals. Even now they were circling him like wolves.

Horst snatched the book out of his hand and read the cover. "You just thought Sherlock Holmes wasn't degenerate English filth?" Horst flung the book into the fire and advanced on Fritz.

"No, I just — I'm sorry. I — " Fritz said.

Just throw the books into the fire, I begged Fritz silently. *They're going to* kill *you if you don't.*

Horst slapped the other books out of Fritz's arms and kicked them away. Before Fritz could recover, Horst shoved him hard with both hands, sending him flying into the Hitler Youth boys behind him. They grabbed him and punched him, like hungry dogs pouncing on rotten meat. "Jew lover!" they cried. "Degenerate!" My face burned hot in the crisp winter air and my hands clenched into fists as the boys fell on Fritz, hitting him, clawing at him, tearing his clothes.

My parents and I had walked away from the Jewish man in the street that Night of Broken Glass four years ago because we had a bigger mission than one man. But I was right here, right now, and I wasn't the helpless little boy I'd been then, and these boys weren't the Gestapo. Then again, I was supposed to stay invisible. I wasn't supposed to get involved.

Fritz dropped to the ground and curled into a ball, the boys kicking him and punching him where he lay, and suddenly I was back in the school yard at St. Paul's, in London, and the older boys were kicking me in the legs, the back, the head, their laughter the only thing louder than my crying. I was helpless. Ashamed. Learning the hardest lesson I'd ever learned:

When you fell down, it was over.

Without giving it another moment's thought, I threw myself into the fight.

THE FIGHTING IRISH

I KICKED SHINS. I ELBOWED STOMACHS. I PUNCHED NOSES
and ears. I stood over little three-cheeses-tall Fritz where he lay on
the ground, protecting him like an antiaircraft gun during an air
raid. I was the only one who came to his defense. But I was enough.
I was a right whirling dervish, a one-man army Hitler would have
given his little mustache to bottle up and ship to the Eastern Front.
Don't get me wrong—those Aryans gave me a busted lip and bruises
that would send Da into a tizzy that night. But at last we reached
an uneasy truce there in the street with the bonfire crackling
behind us. Nobody wanted to come close enough for me to scrape
my knuckles on their faces, and I wasn't moving from the spot.

"He *was* burning books. I saw him," I said, fists clenched,
breathing hard. "He was just taking his time about it. Weren't
you?" I asked Fritz. He still lay on the ground, his arms covering
his head. "*Weren't you?*" I yelled, urgent. If he didn't help me out
here, we were both done for.

"Y-yes," he said at last. "Of course."

Horst stepped in between us and the other boys. "All right. Enough. We can't hurt our Irish guest too badly, boys. Haven't you heard? His daddy is an ambassador. If you break his nose, the Irish might declare war on us!" He pretended to be frightened by holding his hands against his chest and quivering, which got a laugh from the rest of the boys. Ireland was as much a threat to Nazi Germany as a summer rain, and all of us knew it. Horst just loved rubbing it in. I hated him all the more for it, but the joke had broken the bloodlust of the boys, and for that I was grateful. I lowered my fists and nodded my thanks to Horst.

Horst thanked me by cracking a fist across my face and sending me to the ground next to Fritz.

"Compassion is a *weakness*," Horst said for the benefit of me and anyone else in our squad who might not like bullies picking on little kids. "All life is struggle," he added, spouting more lines from the leadership guides the Nazi Party sent him each week. "He who wants to live should fight for himself. He who doesn't want to fight in this world of eternal struggle doesn't *deserve* to live." That part was meant for Fritz. Horst gave him a swift kick to the small of his back to punctuate the lesson, making Fritz writhe. I glared at Horst, wondering what made him such an arse. Maybe Horst really believed all that "might makes right" malarkey. Maybe he didn't like an Irish boy showing up the German "master race."

Or maybe he was just a bleeding maggot.

My money was on the latter. I rose up on an elbow, my Irish blood thundering war drums in my ears, ready to knock Horst's donkey teeth down his throat.

HOW TO TAKE A BEATING

I WANTED NOTHING MORE THAN TO POUND HORST INTO a German pancake. But while the Nazis would give you a medal for punching and kicking your comrades, they'd sack you for attacking a superior officer. And like it or not, that's what Horst was to me in the Hitler Youth. And I wanted to stay in the Hitler Youth—*needed* to stick around, as a spy—so I swallowed my bile.

Horst grinned. It was as though he could see me doing the math of our relationship, could read my powerlessness to fight back. Horst gave Fritz another kick just because he knew I hated it and couldn't stop him. "Above all else, a boy must learn to be beaten," Horst said, quoting Nazi scripture again. "There is no place in Germany for peaceful thinkers and physical degenerates."

I vowed right then and there that one day I was going to teach Horst how to take a beating. But not today. Today I swallowed my rage and helped Fritz to his feet, hoping I hadn't called too much attention to myself.

"And *you*," Horst said. He poked Fritz in the chest. Hard. But his voice was soft. "Someday, when you truly believe in that uniform you're wearing, you won't hesitate. You'll burn books, you'll turn in your parents, you'll *give your life* for Germany. And on that day, you'll finally understand the freedom, the *joy*, that comes with giving yourself completely to the Führer."

A government truck rattled up on the cobblestone street, and two older Hitler Youth boys jumped out of the passenger door before it had even come to a stop. The two boys wore the special insignia that marked them as the SRD, the Hitler Youth's "Patrol Force." The SRD were like junior secret police officers, the Hitler Youth equivalent of the Gestapo. And just as scary. Like the special Hitler Youth army, navy, and marine divisions, the SRD was one of the groups you could apply for after you graduated from the Jungvolk. Most SRD went on to become secret police.

Horst snapped to attention, and so did the rest of us.

"Jungvolk!" one of the SRD boys said. "You are needed at once! A British plane has been shot down just outside Berlin. A parachute was spotted, but no pilot has been recovered. Your help is needed to search the countryside. You are to board the truck immediately!"

A British pilot, on the run in the countryside right outside the city? Fear for his capture made my heart hammer in my chest, but that had to be nothing compared to the real terror he must be feeling right now. If he was caught, he'd be tortured and killed. How long could he hide out from the SS patrols? And if he did elude them, how would he avoid a dozen or more Hitler Youth crawling through the woods and fields to look for him?

The boys in my troop were already clambering for the truck, thrilled to have real work to do for the Fatherland. So much for the rest of the school day — the Hitler Youth had won out over academics yet again. I glanced back down the street, trying to figure out what to do. I had to get word to my parents. They had helped Allied soldiers and spies get out of Berlin before. But the truck was turning around. Boys were filling the benches in back.

"Michael! Come on!" Fritz called from the truck.

I took Fritz's outstretched hand and climbed into the truck just as it rumbled off, leaving behind the bonfire of books. There wasn't time to get word to my parents. I was just going to have to save the British pilot myself.

IN CASE YOU FORGOT

THE TRUCK BUMPED OVER A BRIDGE ON THE WAY OUT OF Berlin, and Fritz rocked into me. I pushed him away with my shoulder. I had already stuck my neck out too far for this kid. I didn't need everybody thinking we were friends.

"Thanks for helping me," Fritz said.

"I didn't help you at all," I said. "Horst says all of us have to learn to take a beating. So I guess I interrupted the lesson."

"I already know how to take a beating," Fritz said. I glanced at his bruises and his cut lip, and I figured he was right. "What I need to learn to do is fight back, like you," Fritz said. "Especially if I'm going to join the SRD and be in the SS one day."

I was stunned. This little guy wanted to be in the SS? And here I thought he hadn't thrown those books into the fire because he was maybe a halfway sane person. Everybody called the SS the Death's Head Squad because of the skull and crossbones on their caps. They wore all black, and they ran the concentration camps and were the people who sent you there. Fritz was crazy if he wanted to join the SS, but then, most German kids were crazy. It was hardly their fault. The Nazis had taken over Germany when they were all just toddlers. Fritz didn't remember any kind of life before Hitler. I had at least had seven years of sanity in Dublin and London before coming to this nutty place. I was the only one who could see how two-faced everything was.

"So, you're English?" Fritz asked.

I bristled at the insult. "*No*. Not English. *Irish*. I hate the English," I told him.

"What's the difference?" Fritz asked.

"Well, for one, the Irish are neutral," I said over the grinding of the truck's gears. "Like Spain, or Sweden, or Switzerland. We're not at war with Germany." People tended to forget that Ireland wasn't part of the United Kingdom anymore — or that we'd only been a part of it in the first place because England had conquered us. For centuries the English had done all they could to take our land, quash our language, and put us in chains, and it took a bloody war for independence to set us free of them.

There were plenty of other ways the Irish were different from the English, chief among them that we weren't a bleeding pox upon the face of the planet. But I didn't want to get into all that with Fritz. I didn't want to be talking to him at all. I had a job to do. I had to get my head back in the game. This was my first chance to do real spy work on my own. Fritz seemed to take the hint, and we rode in silence for the rest of the drive.

The truck pulled to a stop along a dirt road half an hour out-side the city. All around us was farmland, and down a narrow lane sat a farmhouse, barn, and a few small work buildings and sheds. Perfect — and perfectly obvious — places for someone to hide. Off in a field full of haystacks to the west, under the watchful protec-tion of three milk cows, was a flat wrinkly gray thing that must have been the pilot's parachute. You could feel the boys' excitement in the air like the crackle of electric wires in a fog. Everybody wanted to be the one who found the British airman, but nobody more so than me.

We spilled out of the truck and hurriedly formed into rows under the direction of the SRD.

SRD looked different from regular Hitler Youth. Their uniforms were dark blue with special yellow bands on the cuffs that said PATROL FORCE, and when they were on special duty, like they were now, they wore shiny silver gorgets. Gorgets are metal plates that hang down on your chest from a heavy chain around your neck, like a huge, gaudy necklace. Theirs were shaped like six-inch-long kidney beans, with PATROL FORCE written on a banner underneath the double lightning-bolt insignia of the SS, in case you forgot.

The gorgets would have been really silly if they hadn't been worn by the scariest kids in Nazi Germany. The SRD's mission was to watch all the other German kids and turn them in for doing anything illegal. I hated these guys. They ratted out kids for not saluting properly, for violating the nightly curfew, listen-ing to foreign radio broadcasts, sneaking into movies for adults, singing songs they were weren't supposed to sing, and dancing to music they weren't supposed to listen to—all of which could get you sent to a concentration camp. The SRD joined the SS on raids, spied on their neighbors, and monitored church services for anti-Nazi sermons. But their favorite job was the one they were getting to do right now: hunting for Allied airmen shot down over Germany.

Two adult SS officers stepped up to speak to us once the SRD had us in line. Scarier than the SRD, scarier than anything else in Nazi Germany, which was plenty scary enough, were the SS, the Death's Head troops. When people did the German Look to see if anyone was listening, it was the SS they were most afraid they would see over their shoulders.

"The airman is still at large," one of the SS told us, and my heart fluttered with hope. "One group will search to the east, beginning with the farm and moving up into the foothills. The other will search to the west, inspecting the haystacks in the fields before moving into the woods. The pilot *will* be found. Fan out. Cover every centimeter of ground. Leave no place unsearched. Go!"

I was on the team assigned to the farm, and I sprinted toward it faster than anybody.

If I didn't find the British pilot first, he was a dead man.

A PILOT IN A HAYSTACK

I STARTED WITH THE BARN. IT'S WHERE I WOULD HAVE hidden if I'd been on the run. The barn had the itchy smell of stacked hay and cow poops, and was filled with both. I watched my step as I searched for the airman.

Fritz followed me inside, and I sagged. I needed to be alone in case I found the pilot. I couldn't have Fritz or anybody else raising the alarm. I had to lose the kid.

Fritz pulled a pitchfork from a wall of farm tools, and before I could think how to stop him, he jabbed the pointy end into the nearest pile of hay.

I flinched, waiting for a cry of pain from the hiding pilot, but nothing came. Fritz pulled the pitchfork out and attacked another spot. And another. *Jab, jab, jab.* I closed my eyes and flinched every time.

I couldn't stand there and watch, and jabbing at the haystacks was exactly the kind of thing that could keep Fritz busy while

I searched the rest of the barn. I just hoped the pilot was somewhere else.

A rickety old ladder led up to a loft where more hay was stored — an even better hiding place than the haystacks Fritz was poking. But that meant going up.

I held the rung in front of me and closed my eyes. *You can do this,* I told myself. *You* have *to do this. If that pilot's up there, you have to be the first one to find him.* I put a foot on the bottom rung of the ladder, eyes still closed, and my breath came short and quick. I could already feel the familiar tightening in my chest, the sick churning in the pit of my stomach, the dizzy wobbling of my head. *It's not that far. It's not that far. It's not that far.*

I hoisted myself up a rung. And another. And another. I kept my eyes closed the whole time, groping blindly at the rough wood of the hayloft floor when I got to the top. I pulled myself over the edge on my belly, hugging the floor like a toddler clinging to his mother's leg. I was panting now, panicking, and it took me several long seconds to calm down enough to even open my eyes.

As long as I forgot where I was now and didn't look back over the edge, I hoped I'd be okay. I pulled myself to my feet with effort, glad no one had been there to see my pathetic little display. My legs were still wobbly — there was no fooling myself that I was on solid ground, especially up here in this open space — but I wasn't paralyzed with fear the way I got sometimes. It helped to have something else to worry about, and right now, that was finding the missing pilot.

I couldn't risk a German Look over my shoulder to see if anyone was listening, but I was pretty sure I was alone in this part of the barn. "Hello?" I whispered in English. "Are you up here? I'm not German. I'm Irish. I'm here to help."

I waited. Nothing. That didn't mean he wasn't here. He might be here and not believe me. I'm not sure *I'd* believe me. What were the chances of an Irish kid finding you in a hayloft in the middle of Germany?

The hay in the loft didn't look like it had been disturbed since it was stacked up here, but I dug into it anyway, kicking up all kinds of little tickly bits in the air. I sneezed again and again. I couldn't stop sneezing. I was sure I had bits of hay permanently lodged in my nose.

I was also pretty sure the pilot wasn't up here. Which meant I'd gone through all that for nothing.

And now I had to get back down.

I backed warily toward the ladder. I didn't want to look down until I had to, if at all.

"Hey, what are you doing?" Fritz asked.

I turned, startled, and saw Fritz at the top of the ladder.

And the ground ten feet below me.

My head became a helium balloon. The ground floor of the barn dropped away from me, as if I were watching an elevator car plummet down an elevator shaft. The world spun, my body seized up, and I fell over the side.

ACROPHOBIA

FRITZ GRABBED MY SHIRT. I SWUNG OUT OVER THE EDGE, about to drop, but I couldn't move. I was paralyzed. Frozen with fear.

"Michael! Michael, come on! What are you doing? Michael!"

Fritz grabbed my arm, then my body. My weight almost took us both over the side, but Fritz was able to wrestle me back from the edge. We collapsed together on the floor of the hayloft.

The familiar sick and dizzy feeling of vertigo slowly left me as we lay on our backs, panting and exhausted.

"*What happened?*" Fritz asked.

"I'm afraid of heights," I said between breaths.

"Since when?"

"Since before I can remember."

Fritz propped himself up on his elbows to look down at me. "You froze up. You almost fell over the side. You would have broken your neck."

I closed my eyes, trying not to think about it and failing miserably.

"Thank you for catching me."

Fritz stood and offered his hand to help me up. I took it.

"Don't worry," he said. "I won't tell anybody."

It was weird for Fritz to stand there so solemnly and say he wouldn't tell anybody about it. I was embarrassed, sure. Other people climbed up and down ladders and looked out windows all the time without becoming statues and falling over. Why couldn't I? I should just be able to get over it. But it wasn't as if my fear was some horrible secret. Then I realized: In Nazi Germany, every weakness was punished. It was why Fritz was picked on, and why I would be too if the other boys knew about my phobia. They'd forever be hauling me up onto rooftops and forcing me to look over the side. Because that's what Nazi Germany was: the bully who found your most painful wound and poked at it with a stick.

I nodded and shook Fritz's hand. In the heart of enemy territory, without even wanting to, I'd found a friend. But I still hadn't found the missing pilot.

IN WHICH I AM A BLEEDING GENIUS

FRITZ AND I ANNOUNCED THE BARN CLEARED AND CONtinued our search. We were hunting in a hedgerow of shrubs that separated the barn from a cow pasture when I saw it: a spot of blood. Dark red, and still wet. And another. And another. Leading along the hedgerow to the east, up toward the foothills in the distance. And there — a boot print. The airman! He must have been injured in the fall, limped over here, and skirted the hedgerow on his way to higher ground. I quickly kicked dirt over the blood spots as I tried to think what to do.

I had to throw the other searchers off the scent. Send them hunting in the wrong direction. Then I would double back and find the airman myself.

I went back down the hedgerow, away from where the blood trail began and snapped a branch here, a twig there, as though the pilot had run west, toward the haystacks and the forest, not east toward the mountains.

"A broken branch!" I called out, loud enough for the other boys to hear me.

Fritz was the first one there. "He's right! Someone's been this way, and recently!"

An SS officer blew a whistle, and everyone converged on the spot. I ran down the hedgerow, leading the searchers farther and farther away from the blood, secretly snapping a couple of branches along the way. I left those for others to find.

I was feeling pretty good about my brilliant plan to lure the army of hunters in the wrong direction when I stopped to snap another branch and noticed a hint of blue among the mass of brown leaves in the hedge. I parted the branches, and my heart caught in my throat.

Lying on the ground just inside the hedge, right where I'd been leading the entire Nazi search party, was the missing British pilot.

AN ANGRY BADGER

I LET THE HEDGEROW BRANCHES SNAP BACK SHUT AND muttered a short, harsh German word I wasn't supposed to know or say. The British pilot wasn't headed for the hills. He was right here, and I'd led the Nazis right to him! The quick glimpse I'd gotten of him told me he wasn't doing too well, either. He was curled up in a ball as if he was hurt, and he hadn't looked up at me.

"Just stay quiet and still," I told him. "I'm not German. I'm Irish. I'm here to help you." Then I realized I'd said all that in German, which probably hadn't helped. The searchers from the Hitler Youth were getting closer, beating at the hedgerow with rakes and poking into it with sticks. I switched to English and told him the same thing again. "My name's Michael O'Shaunessey," I added.

"Well," came a weak but distinctly English voice from below me, "you can't get much more Irish than that."

"Are you hurt?" I asked him.

"Not at all," he said, even though he was gritting his teeth in agony. "Unless you mean this bloody gash on my arm, or my sprained ankle."

A sprained ankle! No wonder he hadn't made it far.

An SS officer joined the vanguard of Hitler Youth beating at the bushes. He'd be on the pilot in moments. I had to think of something. *Do* something.

"Do you trust me?" I asked the airman, pretending to search the hedgerow.

"Trust an Irishman?" the pilot said. "I'd sooner trust a fox in a henhouse."

"And I'd sooner carry an angry badger across the River Liffey than help an Englishman," I told him.

"Now I know you're Irish. I'm entirely in your hands."

That was a scary thought. I waved Fritz over, hoping he wouldn't see the blue of the pilot's uniform through the brown leaves as I had.

"Come on," I told him, hurrying back the way we'd come. "I think the pilot may have doubled back on us."

"But the trail goes this way," Fritz said.

"Misdirection," I told him. And suddenly I realized that's exactly what the drops of blood had been. The pilot had limped as far as the barn, making it look like he was headed for the hills, then doubled back and hidden in the hedgerow.

"Why would he stay here at the farm? He's had more than an hour to run. He had to head for the hills," I told Fritz. "Let's look for tracks here." I led him right to where I'd found the blood, hoping he'd see it. I didn't want to be the one to cry wolf twice. But of course I'd swept dirt over the blood spots I'd seen, trying to hide them. Idiot!

While Fritz was searching the ground, I snapped a twig off the hedgerow and dragged it across my palm, breaking the skin and bringing blood to the surface. It stung, but that didn't matter. I didn't have long before the searchers found the pilot. I stepped ahead of Fritz and bent down as though searching, squeezing a drop of blood from my clenched fist onto the cold, dry earth. I moved away, squeezing another, and another.

Come on, Fritz, I thought. *See the blood. See the blood!*

I watched the SS officer get closer to the place where the airman was hiding. Closer . . . Closer . . . I was going to have to say something myself—

"Look! Blood!" Fritz cried. "Hey! Hey, I found blood!" he called to the searchers. "A trail of it!"

Hitler Youth boys abandoned their search of the hedgerow and came running. The SS officer stopped right beside where the British pilot was hiding, turned, and then walked back toward us. I heaved a huge sigh of relief. I'd saved the airman, but only for the moment.

"There's more blood here!" a boy cried, finding some in the grass beyond the barn. Blood I hadn't shed. The pilot must have left a longer trail than even I'd seen.

"He's headed for the mountains," the SS officer said, as though he'd always known. He blew his whistle, calling the searchers in the field across the road to join us. "Fan out," he told us. "Form a line. Work your way into the foothills. Find him!"

Fritz joined the growing line of boys and bounded off with them up the hill. I stayed behind, slipping back into the barn while all the other boys from the field joined the search. It felt bad to lie to Fritz, to not tell him the truth about the airman, but I didn't know how much I could trust him yet. I remembered him saying he wanted to join the SRD. The glee he'd shown sticking that pitchfork into the hay in the barn. Was that just the excitement of the chase, or did he really believe all that Nazi claptrap about the master race?

I still had to get the British pilot out of the hedgerow to somewhere safer. But where? I watched the searchers through the gaps in the barn wall until they were over the hill. The hay made me sneeze again, and then I had it.

I knew where to hide the airman.

THE BEFRIENDING BARN

THE BRITISH PILOT WAS TALL, BROAD-SHOULDERED, AND pale, but that last part might just have been because he had a sprained ankle and had lost a lot of blood. He was heavy too. Heavier than I expected. He leaned on me for support as I led him away from the hedge. I didn't know how much of a false blood trail he'd left, or how long we had until the searchers would come running back over that hill, so I picked up the pace.

The airman grunted. "The three-legged race never was my favorite event at the village fair."

"Do you always joke around when your life is in danger?" I asked him as we limped into the barn.

"No better time," he said. He stopped. "This is your idea? Hide me in the barn? I didn't hide in here in the first place because it's the most obvious place to look."

I didn't tell him it was the first place I'd looked for him. But I did tell him it was the last.

"That's why it's the perfect place now," I said. "What better place to hide than someplace that's already been searched and cleared?"

A slow grin spread across the pilot's face. "Very clever. Are you sure you're Irish?"

"You seem like a nice enough fellow," I threw back at him. "Are you sure you're English?"

He laughed and picked up a pitchfork. Together we dug as far back into the hay piles as we could, and I made a little nest for the pilot while he cut a piece of his shirt away to bandage up his arm. There was a lot of blood. Too much. I worried he might bleed to death before we could come back and get him.

"Stay here. My parents will pick you up tonight."

"And just who are your parents? What are you doing here in Berlin?"

"My da is the Irish ambassador to Germany," I told him. "They've helped other Allied pilots get out of Germany. They'll help you too. But they don't even know you were shot down. I had to act fast."

"I'm glad you did," he said, and he shook my hand. This barn was quickly turning into the place where I made new friends. I didn't know a long German word for that, so I made one up: *die Freundschaftserweisungsscheune*. "The befriending barn."

I picked up a pitchforkful of hay and got ready to bury him.

"Wait. I need you to do one more thing," he said. "I took a camera with me from the plane. A big camera. I was taking reconnaissance photos. Very *important* reconnaissance photos. I need you to find the camera. Get the film. It's vital that the film make it out of Germany, even if I don't. I hid it in one of the hay-stacks in the field where I came down."

"Which haystack?" I asked.

The British pilot smiled apologetically.

"Um . . . the brown one?"

EXPOSED

I SEARCHED THE HAYSTACKS FOR HALF AN HOUR BEFORE the search party came back over the hill. I was as empty-handed as they were. It was late in the day. Time to head back to Berlin. Reinforcements from the city had arrived. The search for the airman would continue without us, and my search for the camera would have to wait until I came back with my parents tonight.

"Where were you?" Fritz asked me when we met up back at the truck. "I didn't see you on the search in the hills."

"I thought maybe he'd doubled back a second time, to really throw us off the scent," I lied. "So I searched the haystacks across the road."

Fritz laughed. "You're quite the gumshoe!"

I was surprised he used the word *gumshoe*. It was one of those English words there's no German translation for. If you want to use it, you have to say it in English, and using English words — or words from any other language besides German — was the kind of thing that drew the attention of the SRD and the Gestapo. And how did Fritz know it, anyway? The only place I'd heard it was in American movies, and they didn't show those here anymore.

I didn't have time to ask him about it. The SRD lined us up, and the SS agents spoke to us again. They frowned at us, angry, as if it was our fault the British pilot had gotten away.

In my case, at least, they were right.

"A disappointing day," one of the SS said. "The British spy *will* be captured. Every man, woman, and child in this country is his enemy. He will find no help from anyone."

Well, not every man, woman, and child, I thought. Inwardly, I smiled.

"In the meantime, we have at least found what he came to do."

A cold grin split the SS man's face as he held aloft a large black camera. I sagged. They must have found it when they were searching the field, long before I ever went looking for it.

The SS officer flipped open the back of the camera and yanked out the long plastic filmstrip inside, exposing it to the light and ruining it forever.

A SMALL PROBLEM

IT WAS DARK WHEN MY PARENTS AND I CAME BACK THAT night. The moon was down and the stars were out. Da drove the last mile or so without the headlights on.

"I don't like this," he said.

"Well, I don't much like it either," Ma said. "But we can't just leave the lad there to be captured by the Nazis."

"No," Da said. "I mean I don't like Michael hiding English airmen in barns in broad daylight. He should never have done it."

"And what was I *supposed* to do?" I said, leaning over the back of the front seat. "Just let him get caught?"

"*Yes*," Da said.

I couldn't believe what I was hearing. I couldn't find the words. I looked to my ma in the seat beside him. *She* had to agree with me. She was the real spy in the family.

"He's right, Michael," Ma said. "Sneaking into studies is one thing. Hiding Royal Air Force pilots is another entirely."

"But—but—"

"But nothing," Da said. "What if you'd been caught?"

Ma turned to look at me. "Michael, it's terrible to say so, but sometimes you have to weigh the cost of one man's life against the value of an entire operation."

Suddenly, I was back in the street again during Kristallnacht, hurrying past a man being beaten to death by the Gestapo. Doing nothing. My face burned hot and my heart beat faster.

"It's taken me years to set up my informant network in Berlin," Ma went on. "If you'd been caught, your father would have been expelled and we would have lost everything."

"*That's* what this is about?" I said.

"No, that is *not* what this is about," Da said, scowling at Ma. "It's about Michael getting shot. Or worse."

Only in Nazi Germany was there something worse than being shot. *The concentration camps.*

"Michael, you've a terrific mind for details, and the information you've helped send back has been dead useful," Da said as he drove on. "But you're thirteen years old. You've no business putting your life on the line for anything."

I thought Ma might say something in my defense. After all, she was the one who'd trained with Irish Intelligence since she was sixteen years old. She was the one who had taught me how to come up with an excuse to leave a party, how to slip away unnoticed, how to lie. It was an argument she and Da had all the time. But if she thought different this time, she bit her tongue.

I folded my arms across my chest and stared out the window. *No business putting my life on the line for anything.* That was exactly what was wrong with Nazi Germany. Some of the Germans must have disagreed with Hitler and the Nazis, but they were afraid that if they said something, *did* something, they might get shot. Or worse. So instead of anybody doing anything to help anybody else, they kept their eyes on their feet and pretended the sky wasn't falling down on their heads.

How could none of them *do* anything? How could I *not?*

Da had only allowed me to come along tonight because I knew where the pilot was hidden. He parked the car far down the lane from the farm, and we snuck quietly up to the barn. The farm-hands ought to be sound asleep, and any search for the airman called off till morning, but we still had to be careful.

The barn door creaked so loud I thought for sure they could hear it all the way back in Berlin, but no lights came on in the farmhouse. There was another surprise too: The barn was full of sleeping cows. Da and Ma and I tiptoed between them, careful not to wake them and set them to mooing, which for sure would wake the farmhands. At last we came to the pile of hay where I'd buried the pilot — hopefully not for good.

We dug in the hay with our hands instead of the pitchfork, so as not to spear the airman. But the deeper and deeper we dug, we still couldn't find him. Ma shot me a silent question with her eyes: *Are you sure this is where you left him?* I nodded an emphatic yes. This was where I'd left him, but what if the SS had searched the outbuildings again, not trusting us to do the job? What if they had already captured the British pilot? Was he sitting in some cell in Berlin somewhere right this minute, SS agents interrogating him? Torturing him?

A hand popped up out of the hay beside me, making me jump. He was still there! And he was still alive! My father took the airman's hand and pulled him out while my mother and I brushed the hay from him. He looked worse than before, but Ma would get him fixed up as soon as we got him back to the embassy.

"Did you find my camera?" he whispered to me.

I shook my head. "SS found it first."

He sighed and nodded.

"We can at least get you out of here," Ma said. "You'll have to stay with us a while in Berlin first, until you heal up."

"What's your name, son?" Da asked.

"Lieutenant Simon Cohen, sir," he said, giving us a British salute.

My mother and father froze.

"You're a Jew?" Da asked.

"Afraid so," Simon said, flashing that apologetic smile again. "Is that going to be a problem?"

OUR SUBMARINE

TAKING A JEW INTO BERLIN, THE HEART OF NAZI GERMANY, where Jews were Public Enemy Number One, was indeed a problem. A big one. Berlin wasn't *really* "Jew-free," the way the Nazis claimed. It couldn't be. Anybody with half a brain knew there had to be Jews still in the city, hidden away in secret rooms by sympathetic Germans. The German people even had a nickname for the hidden Jews—they called them U-boats. Like the German submarines. I guess because like U-boats, the Jews were lurking there beneath the surface. The SS were thugs, but they weren't stupid. They knew there were still Jews in Berlin. They just hadn't found them yet. But they were searching for them. Hard. And if the SS discovered you were hiding Jews in your home, you were sunk. Your whole family would be sent off to the concentration camps with them. Taking Simon back to Berlin with us and hiding him in our embassy was super dangerous to all of us. Not to mention it might lead to a major international incident if the Irish ambassador was discovered hiding a Jewish British spy.

We slipped into our home at the embassy around three o'clock in the morning, while all the staff were asleep. Our staff were all German, and though we knew them all by name and they had worked for the embassy for years, Da and Ma still assumed that one or more of them were reporting on us to the Gestapo. Right when we moved here, my parents told me to watch what I said and did around the staff, but that was good advice anywhere in Berlin.

Da and Ma carried Simon to the secret little room in the back of Da's study. It was a tiny space no bigger than a closet, where we hid all the books the Nazis wanted us to burn. Like the missing family in that empty gray house, whoever they were, we had a stash of forbidden books too. I waited there with Simon while Da went for the medicine bag and Ma went to the kitchen for food.

"Well, at least I'll have something to do while I'm holed up," Simon said, looking around at all our forbidden books. "*Murder on the Orient Express. The Dragon Murder Case. The Maltese Falcon*," he said, reading some of the titles. "You've got quite a collection of mystery novels. Which one's your favorite?" Simon asked me.

I shrugged. "I haven't read any of them."

Simon stared at me, flabbergasted. "*You've never read any of them?* You're in a country that is burning piles of books. Books just like these. You're risking your life to stop the Nazis from doing it. You're fighting to give people everywhere the right to do what they want, to read what they want, to think for themselves. This, all this," he said, gesturing at the books on the shelves, "this is what you're fighting for, and *you haven't even bothered to read them?* The Nazis may as well throw them on the fire if you're not going to read them."

I burned red with shame, and I put up my hands in surrender. "Okay, okay!" I said. "Sorry."

"This isn't a game, kiddo," Simon said. "It's a war. And it's not enough to say, 'The Nazis are the bad guys.' It's not *who* you're fighting against that matters. It's what you're fighting *for.*"

Simon pulled a book off the shelf. *The Golden Spiders* by Rex Stout. He put it in my hands.

"We'll start with this one," he said. "Read a few chapters, and then come back every day and we'll talk about it."

I gaped at him. "I already go to school!"

"Where you're taught not one single thing of educational value," Da said, coming back with the medicine bag. "I think it's a brilliant idea."

"Just make sure you don't let the staff see you reading it," Ma said. She'd come back with a sandwich and a glass of milk for Simon.

I groaned and flipped through the pages. It looked boring.

Ma went to work cleaning and bandaging Simon's arm while Da retraced our steps, making sure there were no drops of blood for the staff to find the next day.

Simon hissed with pain as my mother dabbed at his arm with alcohol.

"Did you hear the one about the Englishman, the Scotsman, and the Irishman who were being chased by the Gestapo?" he asked me in a strained voice. There he went, joking again. I figured he was trying to focus on something else besides the pain, so I played along while Ma continued to work.

"I can't say that I have," I told him.

"They hide out in this old warehouse where there are three empty sacks on the floor, and each of them jumps into a sack. The Gestapo officer comes in and sees three full sacks on the floor. He kicks the first one, and the Englishman shouts, 'Woof woof!' The Gestapo man thinks it's just an old dog in the sack, so he kicks the second bag. The Scotsman cries, 'Meow! Meow!' and the officer leaves it alone, thinking it must be a cat. He kicks the third sack, and the Irishman yells, 'Potatoes! Potatoes!'"

"Potato jokes? Really?" I said.

Lieutenant Cohen gave me his big straight-toothed smile. Ma had finished with his arm and was tending to his ankle when Da came back.

"I'll start working on a plan right away to get you out of Germany," Ma told Simon.

"Not you?" he asked Da.

"I'm the legit side of the business," he told Simon. "She's the clandestine part."

Once my parents told me what they were up to, that Night of Broken Glass, I'd begun to see the strange things my mother did in a new light. Like the time when I was seven, just after we'd moved to Berlin, when Ma had taken me for a walk all around the city, shooting my picture in front of the Tempelhof Airport, the German Ministry of Aviation, and the Reich Chancellery, the building from which Adolf Hitler ruled. She hadn't been taking pictures of *me*. Not really. She'd been taking pictures of strategic targets. Even then I'd been part of the family business; I just hadn't known it yet.

"Women and children make terrific spies," Ma told me later. "Because people always underestimate us."

"It will take some time to arrange for the transportation," Ma told Simon now. "But you're not going anywhere until this ankle heals anyhow. You've lost a lot of blood too. A few days' rest and recuperation wouldn't go amiss, I'm thinking."

"What in the name of all that's holy were you doing flying solo over Berlin in broad daylight?" Da asked. American bombers attacked during the day, but there were dozens, hundreds of them at a time. Not solo planes that were easy to shoot at.

"Taking pictures," Simon said. He sucked in air and the color drained from his face as Ma tested his ankle. "Photos ruined, though . . . All for nothing . . . Nazis are developing some new kind of airplane . . . Works without propellers . . . Super fast . . . Caught it on the runway during testing . . . They call it . . . Projekt 1065 . . ."

WAKE-UP CALL

MORNING DAWNED BRIGHT AND EARLY. TOO BRIGHT AND too early when you'd been up half the night rescuing a downed British airman from the countryside and hiding him in your house. I came out of my room and looked down the hall at where my father's study was, thinking about Simon hidden away in that little room. The plan was that Da would lock the door to his study and check in on Simon every few hours, giving him a chance to go to the bathroom, have a little something to eat. But anything more and the staff would know something fishy was happening, and one of them would get word back to the Gestapo.

I watched as the staff came and went, doing their morning chores. Which of them were sympathetic to the Allies? Which of them were loyal to Hitler? Had found "the freedom, the *joy*, that comes with giving yourself completely to the Führer," as Horst called it?

Which of them would spy on us for the Gestapo to save their families from the concentration camps?

There was no way to know. The only thing we could do was to keep our U-boat submerged as much as possible, only letting him up every now and then for air.

I dragged myself to school, half-asleep and fading fast. I planned to close my eyes and sleep through Herr Professor Doktor Major Melcher's lecture on Nazi history. I'd memorized it all already anyway, and could answer anything he asked if he called on me.

I had my head down on my desk at the back of the room before class started, drool trickling from my gaping mouth, when I felt someone poking me in the shoulder.

"Hey! Hey, Michael! Wake up!" It was Fritz. And he wouldn't stop poking me. Yesterday, I had fought to save his life. This morning, all I wanted to do was kill him.

"Leave me alone," I mumbled from behind my arms.

"Michael, wake up! I want to show you something."

I dragged my head up. Whatever this was had better be good.

"I was going to show this to everybody," Fritz whispered, "but I'm just going to show it to you instead." Fritz did the German Look over his shoulder to make sure no one else was listening, and I woke up a little. Whatever Fritz wanted to tell me, he didn't want anybody else to hear it. Which meant it was something worth hearing.

Fritz pulled a big blue piece of paper from his rucksack and pressed it into my hands. He smiled at me, eyes wide, like I should be amazed at what I was seeing. To tell the truth, I didn't understand what I was looking at. Not at first. But when I did, I woke up for good. Fast. It was a secret so big it could change the course of the war. Maybe change the fate of the world.

And I had it right there in my hands.

PROJEKT 1065

THE BIG BLUE PIECE OF PAPER WAS A BLUEPRINT. A TECH-
nical drawing of a new kind of airplane that hadn't been built yet.
An airplane without propellers.

The same airplane Simon had been trying to catch on camera
when he was shot down.

Projekt 1065. It said the name of the project right there in the
corner!

I caught myself doing the German Look to make sure no one
else was watching us.

Fritz was practically hopping. "It doesn't have any propellers,
see? It has two *jet* engines," he said. "It's a new kind of plane. A *jet*
plane! It will go twice as fast as any other airplane in the world!"

Goose bumps crawled up my arms.

"Where did you get this?" I said. I quickly scanned as much of
the paper as I could. There were lines and numbers and detailed
instructions written all over it.

"My father's on the design team," Fritz said proudly. "He'd kill me if he knew I took this from his study. I was going to show the whole troop, but then they beat me up. So I decided I would just show it to you."

I shook my head. I guess sometimes people *did* hand you their secrets. But only if you saved them from getting beat to a pulp.

"Isn't it amazing!?" Fritz was saying. "With this plane, Germany will *smash* the Allies!"

That's exactly what I was worried about. The only reason Hitler hadn't been able to invade England was because of its amazing Royal Air Force, the RAF. They'd beaten the Nazis in the skies over London in the Battle of Britain, fighting against regular old propeller-driven planes with propeller-driven planes of their own. But if this "jet" engine really was twice as fast as any regular airplane, they could fly circles around the RAF. The German Luftwaffe would defeat the RAF, Hitler would invade England, and the Allies would crumble. The Nazis would rule the world.

"This says page one of twelve," I said, my voice no more than a whisper. I tried to hide my desperation. "Where are the rest of the plans?"

Before Fritz could answer, the air was split with a siren so familiar, none of us even jumped.

Air raid.

A JOB TO DO

AS A MEMBER OF THE JUNIOR HITLER YOUTH RANKS, I had a job during air raids — the same job every other Jungvolk had. Each of us had a section of a Berlin street that was "ours," and our job was to run there are soon as the sirens rang and make sure that everyone who lived on that street got to the air raid shelter before the Allied bombs started to fall.

At the sound of the siren, we were all out of our seats and running for the door. Class hadn't even started yet. The Allies were up early today too.

Fritz snatched the blueprint from me and stuffed it back into his rucksack. I caught myself reaching out for it and had to pull my hand back, watching the paper disappear with a gnawing ache like hunger. I *had* to get my hands on the rest of those blueprints. The Allies had to have a jet fighter of their own to survive.

"Talk to you later!" Fritz said as he ran off to do his job.

"You bet you will," I said under my breath. I was going to stick to him now like medals on a Nazi general's uniform.

I ran to my street. Mostly young married women lived there, some of them with babies, others with children in school off doing their own jobs during the air raid. Hardly any men. Most any man old enough to fight was away in the army — or dead. The air raid sirens wailed as I hurried the women and little kids to the shelter underground. I was supposed to shut myself in with them when I was sure we were all present and accounted for, but today I had another person I needed to check in on, and now was the perfect time to do it.

The first bombs started to fall across the city as I ran back to the embassy. I could hear the dull *poom-poom-poom* in the distance, and then the *ack-ack* guns — the antiaircraft guns — began firing back. *Tuf-tuf. Tuf-tuf-tuf.* They were far enough away that I wasn't worried. Besides, I had a deal with the Allied bombers. I didn't shoot at them, and they didn't shoot at me. That was a joke, of course — they had no idea who or what their bombs were hitting when they dropped them from the planes by the ton — but I liked to think it was true.

I ran through empty streets full of empty houses. Anyone could have walked right in and stolen all the silverware, food, radios, anything of value. And sometimes that was just what people did during air raids. People who were poor, or starving, or just looking out for themselves. That was part of the job of the Gestapo and the SRD: to patrol the empty neighborhoods during air raids and make sure nothing was stolen. They took the job very seriously too. The penalty for stealing from houses while everyone was underground in bomb shelters was death.

There weren't any Gestapo or SRD on the street near the embassy when I got there, and I ran up the steps and plowed inside. It was strange to not be met by a servant, to be entirely alone in the house. It was creepy, actually. It felt like everyone in the world was dead and gone except for me.

But of course I wasn't the only person there.

I ran for my father's study and knocked on the door, calling out for Simon. I hoped he was already out of the secret room, walking in circles on his injured foot. Air raids were the only time he could really get out and walk around without anybody seeing him.

Simon unlocked the door and let me in. "Good lord, Michael! You scared the life out of me! What are you doing here?"

"The Nazi . . . jet plane . . ." I stammered, trying to catch my breath. "Projekt 1065 . . . I saw the . . . I saw the blueprints."

SAVING THE WORLD'S BACON

"PROJEKT 1065? *THE BLUEPRINTS?*" SIMON SAID. "HOW the devil did you—?"

I grabbed a pencil and paper from my father's desk and sketched out everything I could remember. I drew the shape of the plane and a few of the numbers and words I'd seen before the air raid siren had sounded and Fritz had ripped the page from my hands.

Simon stared at the paper with an open mouth. "But . . . this is extraordinary! You saw this? Today? When? Where? And how do you remember so much of it?"

I told Simon everything—about Fritz, his father, page one of twelve, my photographic memory.

"I don't believe it," Simon said. "Do you know what this means? I can finish my mission after all—and even better than before! I can bring home actual blueprints, not just photographs taken from twenty thousand feet!" He took me giddily by the shoulders. "You may just save my bacon—and all of England,

America, and Russia's bacon too — if you can get another look at those plans. Can you? And memorize more of them?"

"Sure!" I said. "All I have to do is stay close to Fritz and I'm sure he'll show them to me again. It'll be easy. We're in the same Jungvolk squad and — "

And then it hit me. We wouldn't be for much longer. "Oh. Oh, no."

"What? What is it?"

"I'm not going to be in the Jungvolk anymore. They're calling up all the seventeen-year-old boys from the Hitler Youth to fight in the German army, which means they're promoting all the thirteen-year-olds like me out of the Jungvolk a year early."

"Good lord," Simon said. "Seventeen-year-olds, fighting in the army? The Jerries must be getting pretty desperate. Boys too young to shave, drafted to fight on the front lines." He frowned at me. "But I still don't understand what any of that has to do with buddying up to this boy whose father has the plans."

"The initiation test into the senior Hitler Youth is in less than a week," I explained. "If I don't pass the test, Fritz will join the SRD and I'll never see him again unless he busts me for sneaking into a movie theater. I'll never be able to get close to him."

"And who says you're not going to pass the Hitler Youth initiation?" Simon asked.

"The last test is jumping off a two-story building into a pool," I said. "And I'm afraid of heights. Not just afraid. I mean pee your pants, freeze up, fall flat on your face afraid of heights." Just thinking about the two-story jump made me queasy. "I've tried to get better at it, but — "

"But?"

"But I can't do it," I said meekly.

"Right," Simon said, clapping his hands. "So we have less than a week to get you over your fear of heights, then, eh?"

It wasn't that simple. "You don't understand — " I started to tell him.

"Believe it or not, I do," Simon said. "Look, I've some experience with this. I can help you overcome your fear. Enough at least to pass your test. But to do it, we're going to have to get started right away, all right? Let's head up to the roof."

I quailed. The roof? I couldn't! "D-during an air raid?" I asked. I was more afraid of the rooftop than the bombs falling all around us — *far* more afraid of the rooftop — but I hoped reminding Simon of the air raid would stop this crazy plan.

"Why not?" Simon said. "How else is no one going to see us? Now let's hop to it!"

THE GERMAN BLITZ

BERLIN WAS ON FIRE. THAT'S WHAT IT LOOKED LIKE FROM the roof. Orange-red glows silhouetted the broken shapes of buildings, each inferno sprouting a thick, acrid mushroom cloud of smoke. The air smelled like burning metal and spent firecrackers, tasted like fireplace ash and cement dust. The Americans knew the way to Berlin now as if they were flying from New York to Philadelphia and back, and they dropped their bombs on the city all at once, like children opening their fists to let handfuls of pebbles drop to the ground.

Hundreds of thousands of bombs fell on Berlin, illuminated by the giant German searchlights that swept the dull gray skies for bombers.

The thundering, teeth-clattering explosions of the bombs was accompanied by the staccato *poom-poom-poom-poom-poom* of the Nazis' antiaircraft guns. Yellow streaks shot into the sky, exploding among the planes with pops like fireworks. One of the AA guns in the streets detonated like a cherry bomb, and

I flinched. The searchlights made the guns perfect targets for the bombers they were trying to shoot down.

I had never been outside during an air raid before.

"This is what's going to happen to that factory," I said.

"What factory?" Simon asked.

"The one I stole the secret location for," I said. I told Simon about finding the numbers in the playing card in the automaker's study. "Da sent the message off in the diplomatic pouch this morning. In a few weeks, a few days maybe, British planes will fly over it and do . . . this. I was always so excited to help, but . . . but it won't be soldiers in those factories, will it?"

"No," Simon said. "It'll be prisoners, most likely."

I shrank. I had been worried enough when I thought it would be German civilians, but prisoners? Innocent people? Now they were all going to die. Because of me.

"If we didn't bomb those factories, if we didn't drop these bombs here, today, the Nazis would win, and then there would be even more prisoners. Even more innocent people would die," Simon said. "Sometimes good people have to be sacrificed to win a war."

I nodded. My mother had told me the same thing, in her way, about leaving Simon behind. But we *hadn't* sacrificed Simon, and it was good that we hadn't. How did you decide who to sacrifice and who to save?

"Bad as this is," Simon continued, "the Nazis did ten times worse to us during the Blitz." He spoke quietly, even though it was hard to hear over the explosions. "German planes overhead almost every night, dropping hundreds of thousands of fire-bombs on London. People huddled in Tube tunnels, lying down along the subway tracks. Little kids crying. Babies wailing. And up top, the whole blooming city reduced to rubble. *More than eight months of it.* Fifty-seven nights in a row one time." He paused, watching buildings explode. "Payback. That's what this is."

I knew about the Blitz. Short for *Blitzkrieg*: "lightning war." Poland, Belgium, the Netherlands, Denmark, Norway, France—they had all fallen in a matter of months, sometimes weeks. Sometimes even *hours.*

But Hitler hadn't been able to conquer England. The Battle of Britain, fought entirely in the skies, was supposed to have crippled England and demoralized her people. Made it ripe for an amphibious assault across the English Channel. When it didn't, Hitler gave up on England and turned east toward Russia. England got knocked down and got back up again. But it might not be able to do that a second time if the Nazis developed jet planes.

Which was why I was up here in the first place, I remembered. To get over my fear of—

My stomach seized up as I suddenly remembered where I was. My head bobbed like a barrage balloon. My legs went wobbly, and the rest of me froze. I fell face-first toward the floor of the roof.

OH, CRAP

SIMON PUT A HAND TO MY CHEST, SAVING ME FROM HIT-
ting the deck.

"Whoa there!" he said. "Keep it together, O'Shaunessey. Stay
with me."

I fought to regain control, but I couldn't make my arms and
legs work. My heart worked, though. It worked overtime. It beat
so fast it threatened to overload my system, like a penny stuck
in an electrical socket.

"You stood up here for ten minutes before you remembered
you were two stories up," Simon told me. "That's lesson number
one. Distraction. We have to find something to distract you.
Here—do sums with large numbers. That'll keep your mind
occupied. What's 67,821 plus 91,725?"

Math already paralyzed me when I had my two feet on solid
ground. I closed my eyes and teetered.

"All right, all right, not math!" Simon said. "Come on, then, tell me a joke about what prats the English are. I'm sure you have hundreds."

I shook my head to clear it, but that just made me dizzier. All I wanted to do was to curl up into a ball and pass out. I leaned into Simon, and he had to fall back against a chimney to keep us standing with his sprained ankle.

"Right, then," Simon said, "here's another one for you. An Englishman, a Scotsman, and an Irishman meet a magical fellow at the top of a tall building. The wizard tells them that if they jump off the building, whatever they say while they're falling will appear at the bottom. So the Englishman, he jumps off first, being the bravest of them of course, and he yells, 'Pillows!' and he lands on a big pile of pillows. The Scotsman jumps off next, and on the way down he yells, 'Hay!' and he lands in a big pile of hay. Last up is the Irishman, but he trips on the edge of the building right as he's about to jump, and as he falls he yells, 'Oh, crap!'"

I laughed in spite of myself.

"There we go!" Simon said. "You hate the English, right? Of course you do—you're Irish. So every time you start to lose control, you think of some insult to throw at me, whether I'm there or not. That'll give you something else to focus on."

It was a good idea, but I was too far gone. My stomach heaved. I leaned over and threw up my breakfast and collapsed into a heap on the rooftop.

Simon slid down with me. "Well, we'll just have to keep working at it, won't we?" He sat with me while I fought to stay conscious. "So, funny story," he said. "I'm deathly afraid of something too. And you'll never guess what."

A SCREAM OF SWIFTS

"*BIRDS*," SIMON SAID. "THAT'S WHAT I'M AFRAID OF. BIRDS."

I looked up at him. Bombs and antiaircraft tracers still flared and boomed all around us, and Simon didn't bat an eye at them. But he was afraid of *birds*?

"My hand to God," Simon said. "Birds frighten the pants off me. One bird I'm all right with, though I'm still not a fan. But get a group of them together, all lingering about in a tree or on an electrical wire . . ." He shuddered. "A murder of crows kills me. A pandemonium of parrots makes me panic. A bevy of quail makes me quail. Which is ironic, don't you think? Seeing as how the birds and I both love to fly. I once almost crashed a de Havilland twin-engine Mosquito just trying to get away from a row of geese flying south for the winter."

I chuckled.

"My father was a hard man," Simon said, his eyes on the bombers in the sky. "Solicitor. Very serious. Didn't take it lightly that his son had some irrational fear of a bunch of birds. Told me the best thing for it was to confront my fear head-on. So one evening he took me up onto a rooftop much like this one and stood me on a chimney. He told me it was to get used to birds. What he didn't tell me was that the chimney was full of swifts."

I sat up and wiped my mouth with my sleeve.

"Have you ever seen swifts emerging from a chimney, Michael? At a precise time each evening, they burst forth from the chimney where they nest, like water from a garden hose. Hundreds of them at a time. They battered me, clawed me, flapped their terrible wings in my face as they hurtled by. I was absolutely surrounded by them. I tried to leap away, but my father grabbed me by the shoulders and held me in place. Made me stand there and be swarmed by them. The idea was that by facing my worst fear, I would just . . . get over it."

There was a haunted look in Simon's eyes now, and I knew he wasn't joking. About any of it. It sounded silly to be afraid of birds, but a real fear, a real phobia, was a serious thing. People without one couldn't understand.

Simon worked at steadying his breathing. Was he doing sums in his head to distract himself? Whatever he was doing, I gave him the time and space to do it.

"Didn't work, of course," Simon said when he had recovered a little. "I think I can confidently say it made things very much worse. So I won't be dangling you off the side of the building, in case you were wondering. But confronting your fear in a controlled situation and learning to deal with your responses helps prepare you for the big ones. To that I can attest. Small steps, Michael. Small steps."

All around us, the Allies pounded Berlin, leveling the city to rubble a little more.

"So, ready to try again?" Simon said at last. "I think the Yanks will give us another hour or so's privacy."

I took a deep breath and nodded. "Did you hear the one," I said, "about the Irishman, the Scotsman, and the Englishman stranded on a desert island?"

THE EDELWEISS PIRATES

THE AFTERNOON AFTER THE AIR RAID, A DARK BLACK cloud hung over the bombed-out city. Gray ash still fluttered in the air like snow. Tumbled bricks and broken furniture filled the streets. Hitler Youth boys and aging air wardens were already hard at work, spraying water on the flames, tossing rubble into wheelbarrows, and stacking up the bodies of the people who hadn't made it to the air raid shelters in time. More Hitler Youth stood guard over shops and banks. A little boy in gray trousers and a little gray coat sat on a shattered roof timber, clutching a teddy bear and crying softly. He couldn't have been more than four years old. A girl from the Bund Deutscher Mädel, the girls' version of the Hitler Youth, came and collected him. There was no sign of his parents. It was a scene that had played out the day before, and the day before that, and the day before that. Except today there was something new.

I stopped in front of a crumbling wall and stared. DOWN WITH HITLER! was painted on the wall in big red letters. Beside it was written THE HIGH COMMAND LIES! DOWN WITH THE NAZI BEAST! And underneath the words was a little painted stencil of an edelweiss flower.

Edelweiss is a mountain flower with white petals in a kind of star shape around a yellow fuzzy center. The stems and leaves are fuzzy too, and they grow pretty close to the ground. The Germans and Swiss and Austrians were mad for them, because edelweiss only grow in high altitudes, where other plants can't grow. Survival of the fittest, flower-style. Tough but "pure." That made them holy around here. So holy that they were claimed as a symbol by both the Nazis and what passed for the resistance in Berlin: the Edelweiss Pirates.

That's what they called themselves. Kids the same age as the Hitler Youth who didn't agree with Hitler and the Nazis. Like the real edelweiss, they grew up in a hostile place that was always trying to kill them. They were dropouts—from school, from the Hitler Youth, from society. They spent their days avoiding the SRD in cafés and beer halls, smoking cigarettes and playing pool and making up funny lyrics to Hitler Youth songs. They let the air out of car tires, stole bicycles, picked fights with the Hitler Youth when they caught one of them alone. But ever since the defeat at Stalingrad, the Pirates had gotten more serious. Now they were coming out during air raids when hardly anyone else was around and painting anti-Hitler slogans all over the city. If they weren't careful, they were going to wake the sleeping bear. But I was glad somebody else was doing something to fight back.

A REAL NAZI

THE NEXT MORNING, I MADE A DETOUR BY FRITZ'S HOUSE on the way to school. Most of the buildings on his street were still standing, and red-and-white flags with big black swastikas hung from every windowsill. Some people may have agreed with the Edelweiss Pirates, but they weren't brave enough to show it.

Fritz came to the door when I knocked. I hoped he would invite me inside, hoped I might get a chance to snoop for the blueprints of Projekt 1065, but he told me to wait on the front step and came back with his rucksack and his little sister. Her name was Lina. She was ten years old, wore her blond hair in braids like every other girl in Berlin, and was dressed in the uniform of the junior BDM: a blue skirt, a white blouse, and a honey-colored jacket.

Lina froze when she saw me. She stared at me with big saucer-shaped eyes.

"What?" I asked her. But Lina didn't say anything. She kept staring at me with those big round eyes as she followed us to school.

"Your sister is creepy," I told Fritz.

"I know. She's a goofy dame."

I shot Fritz a sideways look. *Goofy dame* was more English slang, like *gumshoe*. I didn't want to scare him off, so I didn't say anything about it. But I filed it for later.

"So, do you still want to join the SRD?" I asked Fritz. The Hitler Youth initiation was in three days.

Fritz nodded. "I don't know if I'm going to make it, though," he said. "I'm not strong enough. Not fast enough. Not tough enough."

"Well, maybe we can help each other out," I told him. "I want to be in the SRD too." I hated the idea of being in the junior Gestapo, hated the thought of marching around in jackboots and spying on my neighbors. But if it meant staying close enough to Fritz to get to the jet fighter plans, I'd do it. "We can train together. I can help you get stronger. Teach you to fight. And . . . maybe you can help me get over my fear of heights. For the test of courage."

"It's a deal!" he told me, and we shook hands.

To beat Hitler, I was going to have to become a real Nazi.

SEAT MEAT

"YOU'RE IN MY SEAT."

Fritz and I had just sat down at desks in our classroom. Another boy, named Willi, stood over Fritz, demanding he give up his desk. Willi was bigger and stronger than Fritz, but then, *every* boy in the class was bigger and stronger than Fritz.

Fritz started to get up, but I caught his eye and shook my head. If he was going to learn to be tougher, he was going to start right now.

Fritz froze. I could see the fear, the doubt, pass over him like a cloud. But he really must have wanted to join the SRD bad. He slowly sat back down in his seat, his eyes lowered.

"I said, *you're in my seat,*" Willi repeated. He gave Fritz a slap that made his head turn.

"Sock him," I whispered. It was English slang, but Fritz understood.

Fritz clinched his fist, screwed his eyes shut, and swung. He landed a punch right to Willi's gut, doubling him over.

"You little runt!" Willi cried. He threw himself at Fritz, and they tumbled into the aisle.

"Hit him!" I told Fritz. "Kick him!" In seconds the whole class was there, cheering them on. None of the rest of them cared about Fritz or Willi. They just wanted to see some blood.

It was hard to watch. Fritz was a terrible fighter. He flailed about, hardly ever landing a punch. I think he may have even hit himself in the head. I wanted to pull Willi off him, to do the fighting for him, but that wasn't going to teach Fritz anything.

"What is this?" Herr Professor Doktor Major Melcher cried. He pushed his way through the watching boys and grabbed Fritz and Willi by the ears. "Fighting. Always fighting! That's all you monsters over do! It's what you're bred to do. To fight and die for the Führer!"

I blinked. Herr Professor Doktor Major Melcher wasn't saying anything we hadn't heard before. Half the stories we read in our primer were about German boys who fought and died for the Fatherland. The very motto of the Hitler Youth was "We are born to die for Germany." But there was something in the way Herr Professor Doktor Major Melcher said it. Like he didn't believe in what he'd been teaching us anymore. Like maybe he never had.

"Sit down! All of you." He flung the two boys away so hard I thought he was going to rip their ears off. I had never seen Herr Professor Doktor Major Melcher this mad before.

Fritz slid back into his seat, and Willi slunk away. I was worried Fritz would be upset at the beating he took, but when he turned to look at me his eyes were alive and he was grinning wolfishly. He was drunk on confidence. Even though he'd taken a beating, he liked the feeling of fighting back.

"Sit down and shut up, or I'll beat you until you can't sit down!" Herr Professor Doktor Major Melcher said. A boy in the first row sneezed, and Melcher gave him a wicked smack with his ruler. I was so startled I sat up straight in my chair. Herr Professor Doktor Major Melcher had always been snappish, but this was different. I could feel the atmosphere in the room grow colder, the eyes of the boys in the class grow narrower. They *were* monsters, all of them, and monsters didn't like to be bitten by other monsters.

Herr Professor Doktor Major Melcher began class by handing back essays we'd turned in a few days ago titled "The Educational Value of the Reich Labor Service." Bor-ing. There was a lot of grumbling as people got their grades this time, though. Mine was a D. I blinked in amazement. I'd never gotten such a bad grade on an essay before — mostly because I copied all my essays straight from stupid Nazi propaganda, just like I'd done for this one. Giving me a D on words I'd lifted right out of the German newspapers was like Herr Professor Doktor Major Melcher saying he disagreed with the official party line. And he did *not* want to be admitting that in front of a class full of boys who made it their business to rat people out to the Gestapo.

There were a lot of questioning looks between the boys before Melcher told us to open our biology textbooks to the next chapter. The page had a picture of a healthy Aryan man with good posture standing next to hunchbacked, ugly-looking *Untermenschen* — "subhumans" like Jews, Poles, Russians, and Africans.

I slid down in my seat, ready for another ridiculous lecture on the superiority of the German "master race." I had what the Germans would call good *Sitzfleisch*. It literally translated as "seat meat." It meant being able to sit through something long and boring, as if you had a big padded butt.

But today's lecture wasn't boring. In fact, what Herr Professor Doktor Major Melcher said had all of us sitting up in our seats.

CULTURE DESTROYERS

I KNEW SOMETHING WAS UP WHEN HERR PROFESSOR Doktor Major Melcher told us to put away our textbooks. "We don't need these things," he said, dropping his in the wastebasket. That caused more looks between the boys.

"We know the truth, don't we, students?" Herr Professor Doktor Major Melcher said. "Tell me — what does the ideal Aryan look like? The perfect example of the master race."

Aryan was Nazi code for Western European white people — of which the Nazis were the perfect example, of course. Boys raised their hands and gave the answers that had been drilled into them. Aryans had blond hair. Blue eyes. Square shoulders. Smooth straight noses. Square jaws. Above-average height. Superior strength, intelligence, and agility, with pure Aryan ancestors as far back as six hundred years.

"Good, yes," Herr Professor Doktor Major Melcher said. "Like our beloved Führer, yes? The Aryan ideal!" He pointed to the picture of Adolf Hitler on the wall behind him. "Our Führer, who has dark hair and dark eyes. Whose nose is bulbous, who is short and never takes physical exercise. And where is his grandfather from? Czechoslovakia, perhaps? Poland? He has never told us. Hmm. So perhaps not the best example."

You could almost hear the classroom gasp. Was Herr Professor Doktor Major Melcher joking? It had to be a joke. It was no secret that the Führer didn't match the Aryan ideal that he'd gone to war to defend, but no one talked about it. To speak of it in public was like saying the emperor wasn't wearing any clothes. It just wasn't done. But Melcher wasn't joking, I could tell, and so could the other boys. I felt as though I could hear the heartbeats of every boy in the room but mine slow to a cool, calculated thrum. They were trained to be on the lookout for dissenters, people who didn't agree with the Nazi Party, tuned in like the special radios the Nazis sold that only picked up German radio stations.

"But the Führer is exceptional," Herr Professor Doktor Major Melcher said, and the room relaxed slightly. He could still get out of this if he praised Hitler and went back to teaching the party line. "Surely the other Nazi leaders are true Aryans!" he said. "Herr Himmler, head of the SS! Shortsighted. Dark hair, dark eyes. No chin. Nose like the beak of a bird. No, perhaps not. Propaganda Minister Joseph Goebbels, then! Short of stature, thin, acne-marred face — ah, and that clubfoot. Hardly the Aryan ideal. Can anyone think of a Nazi leader who *does* match the Aryan ideal our young men are fighting and dying for? No?"

Herr Professor Doktor Major Melcher was met with a wall of silence. The boys sat watching him the way hawks stared

unblinkingly at their prey. The only time I'd been more frightened for another person was when I'd seen the Jewish man being
beaten on Kristallnacht.

I was sweating and shaking as though it was me up there in
front of the class, digging a grave for myself. It was like a nightmare I couldn't wake up from. I had no idea what had happened
to Herr Professor Doktor Major Melcher, what had made him
change his mind or finally tell us what he'd always secretly been
thinking. But if he wasn't careful, he was going to end up in a
concentration camp.

"Remember what we learned last week?" Herr Professor
Doktor Major Melcher went on. "Every race in the world can be
sorted into one of three categories: culture founders, culture maintainers, and culture destroyers. Aryans, of course, are the culture
founders and maintainers. Every great advancement in the history
of mankind has been made by Aryans! Like paper. Ah, no, wait.
That was invented by the subhuman Chinese. Gunpowder too. The
radio! No—an Italian. The gramophone—no, a German Jew! But
I'm sure we can think of something."

A number of the boys started to call out Aryan advancements,
but Herr Professor Doktor Major Melcher waved them away.
"No matter who created these things, we must defend them
against the culture *destroyers*, yes? For what do culture destroyers
do? They burn books. They ban music. They rip great art from
museum walls. They refuse to teach literature, music, and art to
their children. They are monsters!"

I held my breath. No one spoke. The Nazis had done all those things in the name of "preserving" the pure Aryan culture, and we all knew it. I gripped the edge of my desk, worried for Herr Professor Doktor Major Melcher. Like the Edelweiss Pirates, he was finally standing up to the Nazis and telling the truth.

And it was going to get him killed.

The bell rang. It was time for the first of our five Hitler Youth–mandated hours of physical education in our eight-hour school day.

The boys in the class stared mutely at Herr Professor Doktor Major Melcher as they filed past. They were giving him the silent treatment. The forty thirteen-year-old boys in our class had never left the room so quietly. It was spooky. Herr Professor Doktor Major Melcher had to notice.

"Just remember," he called to us, "you are members of the master race! It is your God-given duty to bring order to this wicked world by dying for your Führer!"

FOR THE FÜHRER

AFTER SCHOOL, FRITZ AND I TRAINED FOR THE HITLER
Youth initiation in an alley near his house. I stood on top of a
tallish pile of rubble from a bombed-out wall, trying to practice
breathing slowly. Fritz was running sprints up and down the alley,
dodging the debris that littered the street.

"Herr Professor Doktor Major Melcher really put his foot in it
today," Fritz said as he ran by.

It was hard to talk and focus on my breathing at the same time,
but Melcher was a welcome distraction. "He's crazy. He's going to
get himself taken into protective custody," I said.

Protective custody was one of those terms everybody in Germany
used with a wink and a nod. When the Gestapo picked you up for
doing something wrong, they made you sign a piece of paper officially *asking* them to take you away—for your own protection,
they said. But what you really needed protection from was the
Gestapo.

I wondered again why Fritz wanted to be in the SRD, the junior Gestapo. So I asked him.

Fritz ran in silence for a few moments before answering. "For Germany," he said at last. "For the Führer. Everything I do is for the greater good of the Fatherland."

It was the party line. Propaganda. Did he really believe that? Even if he did, I felt like there was some other reason he was so determined to make the SRD. He could have been part of the regular Hitler Youth without any effort. What was it that made him want to be in the super-elite Patrol Force?

A LOCKED-ROOM MYSTERY

MY *SITZFLEISCH* GOT ANOTHER WORKOUT THAT NIGHT sitting through another boring state dinner. Part of my father's job was to go to meetings with important government officials, but another part of his job was to invite Nazis to the embassy for fancy meals.

The embassy where a Jewish RAF spy was hiding in the next room.

It was all I could think about while the Nazis around me talked about factories and battles and the Edelweiss Pirates. Simon, folded up in that tiny little closet. Had he gotten out again since the air raid that morning? Had he had anything to eat? Had a chance to go to the bathroom?

Suddenly, I realized everyone was looking at me expectantly. Someone must have asked me a question.

"I—I'm sorry. I'm not feeling well," I said. "May I please be excused?"

My mother gave me a look from the other end of the table. I knew what that look meant: The best way to keep Simon hidden and safe was to pretend that nothing was different, to smile and laugh and be the good little Hitler Youth at the dinner table. But she took pity on me with a sigh.

"Take your plate with you," she told me. "In case you're hungry later."

Take a plate for Simon, she meant! She knew exactly where I was going. I collected my plate and my drink, nodded my apologies to the Nazis at the table, and went for the hall.

"His German is so good!" I heard a woman say as I left. "If I didn't know you were Irish . . ."

I did the German Look, saw no one was watching, and slipped into my father's study. I put the food on his desk, locked the door, and went to the corner with the secret room.

"Simon," I whispered. "It's Michael."

I found the hidden latch that opened the bookcase and pulled on it. The bookshelf swung open, and Simon pulled himself to his feet, unfolding his lanky arms and legs like a map.

"Boy am I glad to see you," he said. "I have to see a man about a horse." He hightailed it to the private bathroom off my father's study, and I waited while he relieved himself.

"We have to be quiet," I warned him when he came out. "Ma and Da are hosting a dinner party. The dining room's crawling with Nazis."

"Foxes in the henhouse, eh?" he said, falling on the food I'd brought him. "There's no potatoes!" he said around a bite, joking again about the Irish and their love of potatoes.

"Didn't you hear?" I said. "There was a potato famine a hundred years ago."

The truth was, even though we were in an embassy and could afford the best of what was available, the war made food as scarce here in Germany as it was back in the British Isles, and we both knew it.

"Did you get inside his house?" Simon asked between hungry bites of bread.

He meant Fritz, of course. The jet fighter plans. I shook my head. "But I think I'm getting closer. We trained after school. After we did some exercises, I taught him how to fight."

"Fighting. The other Irish pastime," Simon said. "After drinking, of course."

"We wouldn't have gotten so good at either one without the English as neighbors," I told him.

Simon lifted his cup of tea to me in salute. He enjoyed our verbal sparring as much as I did. I smiled. The other Catholic families we had known in Dublin were big, lots of sons and daughters, and in my daydreams I had an older brother who would joke with me, wrestle with me, stay up late with me discussing deep thoughts. Defend me when the bullies ganged up on me in the school yard. For a moment, I imagined Simon like part of our family, saw a future, long after the war, where we were great friends who got together in London pubs to talk about our jobs, our families, what books we were reading.

"I finished *The Golden Spiders*," I told him.

Simon swallowed down a too-big bite of bread. "Already? Not too painful, then, I take it?"

"It was great," I said. And it really had been. It was about a boy in New York who sees a woman in a car call for help, a woman wearing earrings that look like golden spiders, and he goes to the famous detective Nero Wolfe and his assistant, Archie Goodwin, for help. "I like Archie a lot," I said. "Wolfe's smart, but he's a jerk."

Simon laughed. "Yes, he is. What was your favorite part?"

We talked about the book for a few more minutes while Simon inhaled what was left of the food and drink.

"I think next," he said, going back inside the little closet with all the forbidden books, "we'll try something by Agatha Christie." He scanned the shelves, looking for the book he wanted. "A locked-room mystery." He smiled and gestured at his tiny apartment. "Seems appropriate. Or no, wait — here. *The Maltese Falcon.* You'll love this one."

Suddenly the doorknob to Da's study turned. The door cracked open. I flung the secret bookshelf door closed on Simon and threw myself backward against it to make sure it was closed as someone knocked and stuck his head inside the door.

SS-OBERSTURMFÜHRER TRUMBAUER

IT WAS ONE OF THE NAZIS FROM DINNER. SS-Obersturmführer Trumbauer, the man I'd sat beside at the automaker's dinner. A man whose job was to find the Jews still hidden in Berlin.

"Hello?" SS-Obersturmführer Trumbauer said. "I was looking for a telephone."

My heart raced, and my chest heaved as if I'd just run a marathon. I could have sworn I locked that door!

"Ah, there's one," Trumbauer said, spying the phone on my father's desk. He went to it, picked up the receiver, and told the operator the number he wanted. He watched me like a cat while he waited.

"I-I just came in to find something to read," I said. I held up *The Maltese Falcon*, then realized it was a banned book and quickly hid it behind my leg. This was a disaster. Had he seen the title of the book?

SS-Obersturmführer Trumbauer smiled faintly. "You really do look peaked," he said, still staring at me. I could feel myself sweating from the roots of my hair. He looked down at the empty plate of food on the table. "But at least you have your appetite back."

He was playing with me. I was sure of it. He knew Simon was here, and he was playing with me. I started to panic. What should I do? Call for my mother? And what would *she* do? Drug *him* too? An SS official, at a state dinner at the Irish embassy?

"Yes," Trumbauer said into the phone. His call had been put through by the operator. "One moment." He looked up at me. "If you would excuse me?" He wanted to be alone. To talk on the phone, or to search for Simon?

I peeled myself off the bookcase and walked stiffly across the room.

"I hope you feel better," SS-Obersturmführer Trumbauer called to me as I left. "We need more boys like you to join our cause if we're to succeed."

But I didn't feel better. I felt worse. And I wasn't going to feel any better until I was sure Simon was safe.

ADMITTANCE DENIED

PENNANTS WITH THE WORDS FIGHT!, SACRIFICE!, AND TRIUMPH! emblazoned on them fluttered in the cold February breeze. The day of the Hitler Youth initiation tests was bright and clear, the gray clouds of winter parting to reveal an almost blindingly blue sky. It had been two days since the dinner party. Two days since I was sure SS-Obersturmführer Trumbauer had come into my da's study looking for Simon. But if the Nazi had gone looking for him that night, he hadn't found him, and in the days that followed, the Gestapo hadn't knocked down our door and come tromping in to arrest Simon — or us. Maybe in my fear of getting caught, I was imagining things, but my visits to Simon in the interim to talk books had been shorter and more cautious.

SS-Obersturmführer Trumbauer's words echoed in my ears: *We need more boys like you to join our cause if we're to succeed.* If I had really believed in Nazi Germany, if I had really thought, the way some Germans did, that Adolf Hitler was sent by God to save the German people and rule the world, I might have believed today's beautiful weather was a sign. An omen. I might have believed this was what they called Führer weather — the way the rain and snow and clouds seemed to miraculously disappear any time something important happened, like the annual party rally in Nuremberg, or the Berlin Olympics in 1936, or whenever Hitler gave a speech. As though God was winking at Nazi Germany.

But I was pretty sure God didn't have anything to do with Nazi Germany.

Fritz and I stood together in line, waiting to enter the testing ground. Did Fritz really believe the Nazi propaganda? And what about all these other boys? How many of them really *wanted* to be Nazis when they grew up, and how many of them hated all this nonsense but had to join because it was the law? You never knew the real Nazis from the fake ones, and you couldn't exactly ask. Everybody had to pretend to be excited about the initiation even if they weren't, for fear of the SRD spies who walked up and down the line. The junior Gestapo that Fritz was so desperate to join. And me along with him.

The boy ahead of us in line was stopped by one of the SRD. Apparently, his father had been heard making jokes about Hitler in a beer hall one night, and neither of his parents were members of the Nazi Party. The Jungvolk boy made excuses, but the SRD boy cut him off.

"You will not be permitted to continue in the Hitler Youth

until this situation is satisfactorily resolved," the SRD boy said. "Admittance denied."

I thought the boy had gotten off lucky, but he ran away in tears. Either he was one of the true believers, or he just knew he had no future in Germany if he wasn't in the Nazi Party.

Fritz gave me a horrified look. Getting kicked out of the Hitler Youth was his worst nightmare.

I was next. I hated Hitler and the Nazis, but I still held my breath and prayed I wouldn't be sent away. I shouldn't have worried. My parents couldn't be in the Nazi Party because they were foreign diplomats, and I could trace my family line far enough back that I was declared genetically "pure" enough. Fritz too.

We were in. All we had to do now was pass the tests.

UNFIT TO LIVE

FIRST UP WERE THE "INTELLIGENCE" TESTS, WHICH WE both passed easily. We recited facts about Hitler's first glorious yet illegal attempt to overthrow the German government in 1923. Quotes from *Mein Kampf*. "Evidence" of the Nazi biological theories. More propaganda about how the Führer had saved Germany from the humiliation and economic depression of losing World War I.

I remembered all of it the way I had remembered the words and numbers on the Projekt 1065 blueprints with only a glance. It made me sick to my stomach to repeat all the Nazi lies as facts, made me want to scream that none of it was true and every brown-shirted boy among us was the world's biggest joke, but I had to remember why I was doing this — to get close enough to Fritz to see the rest of those plans.

The physical tests were much more demanding, particularly for Fritz. Each Hitler Youth candidate had to meet minimum requirements in different events, and SRD candidates were expected to be among the best. We had to run 60 meters in twelve seconds, long jump 2.75 meters, and throw a softball 25 meters. I did all these with ease, and spent the rest of the time rooting for Fritz. He struggled to meet the minimums, but he was running, jumping, and throwing faster and farther than he ever had before. He had a wild look in his eyes, like he refused to fail. Like he wanted this more than any other thing he had ever wanted in the world. I wondered again what was driving him to not just be promoted within the Hitler Youth, but to want to be in the SRD. Most everybody else dreamed of ending up in the Air Hitler Youth, the special youth division of the German air force, where you got to fly gliders and train to be a pilot.

One boy was even weaker than Fritz. He clearly had asthma, and by the time we got to the gymnastic tests he was so out of breath he couldn't go on. He begged for another chance, begged for time to get his breathing under control, but the Hitler Youth boys in charge of the tests were merciless. "You aren't fit to be a Nazi," they told him, "which means you are unfit to live!"

I saw a flicker of doubt dull the wild look in Fritz's eyes as the asthmatic boy ran away, gulping down tears. I knew Fritz was imagining himself failing the physical tests and sobbing all the way home. He was so wound up about all this, I worried he would kill himself if he didn't make it. I put a hand on his shoulder. "Come on," I told him. "We've trained for this. You can do it. Both of us can."

Fritz nodded, and the steel came back to his gaze. He had done better than either of us had expected, but we both knew he wasn't in the clear yet. The real test for me was still to come — the dive off the two-story tower into water. But the real test for Fritz came first.

The boxing test.

THE NAZIS' SECOND-FAVORITE SPORT

FRITZ AND I WATCHED AS TWO BOYS PUNCHED AND jabbed at each other in a little makeshift boxing ring. When kids weren't performing their physical tests or cheering for their friends, this was what they all came to watch. Boxing was the one thing where you could demonstrate the glorious "spirit of aggression" and "overcome your fear of pain" all at once. After invading defenseless countries, it was the Nazis' second-favorite sport.

"It all comes down to who they pick to fight you," I told Fritz. One of the two boys in the ring was bigger than the other, and was giving his opponent a right beatdown. The boy in charge of the pairings and evaluations was our old friend Horst, the sadistic boy who'd been the leader of our Jungvolk group. He smiled like a donkey as the big kid knocked the little kid to the ground and kept beating him while he was down. Horst hated Fritz for his weakness, and was sure to give him the biggest, meanest opponent he could.

Something in the boy on the ground went *crunch* from a blow from the bigger boy, and the color drained from Fritz's face.

"Just remember what I taught you," I told him. "Keep your legs apart so you don't get knocked down as easy. When you fall down, it's over. Keep your weight on your back foot. Turn sideways so there's less of you to hit. Tuck your chin, keep your elbows in, and your hands up. No hooks. No uppercuts. They take too long. Short, straight jabs."

Three days wasn't enough time to teach someone how to really fight, but I hoped it was enough for Fritz to at least survive. That's all he was hoping for too. He took up the stance I'd taught him and practiced a few jabs while the previous loser was carried out of the ring.

"All right, let's see who's next," Horst said, consulting his clipboard. "Ah! Fritz Brendler!" His eyes lit up with the anticipation of violence. "And who will we choose to fight you?" His hungry eyes swept the crowd, stopping on the biggest and toughest-looking boy of them all. He was a head and a half taller than Fritz, with arms thicker than Fritz's neck, and a crooked nose that said he'd been in more than his fair share of fights.

I thought I heard a squeak come out of Fritz.

"Fritz Brendler, your opponent is..." Horst announced, drawing it out, "Michael O'Shaunessey!"

AN EASY FIGHT

I WAS STUNNED. *ME,* FIGHT *FRITZ*? NO!

"That's right, mick," Horst said, giving me his donkey-toothed smile. "No more fighting little Three-Cheeses-Tall's battles for him. Now he has to fight *you*!"

I thought Fritz would be freaking out, but he just nodded at me and climbed calmly into the ring. Then I realized why he was so unfazed. Horst had made a huge mistake! He thought we were going to beat each other senseless, but now we could take it easy on each other. We would put on a good show, each get in one or two light jabs, and then we'd be done — and Fritz wouldn't have to take a beating from one of the animals who smelled fresh blood.

We tied on our boxing gloves and circled each other, pretending to look for openings. I nodded and smiled slightly at Fritz to let him know I understood.

Bam! Fritz hit me with a hard right jab that snapped my head back and made me see bright spots in my eyes. The boys around us cheered and laughed. Watching the Irish "mick" get beat up was second only to watching the little runt Fritz get beat up. This was high entertainment.

Bap-bap! Fritz fired another right jab and followed it up with a left, just like I'd taught him, but this time instinct took over and I blocked the shots with my gloves.

"What are you doing?" I whispered.

Fritz didn't answer. He came at me again, raining a hail of punches on me. *Bap-bap-bap-bap-bap!* He never punched hard enough to get through my defenses, but it wasn't for lack of trying. Fritz was throwing everything he had at me. Any idea that we were going to take it easy on each other was out the window, and soon everybody on the field was clustered around us, jeering us on.

I kept my gloves up, defending against his attack without taking a swing, and the crowd booed me. "Just what I thought," Horst yelled. "The mick's soft! Looks like he's not going to pass his boxing test."

I heaved an exhausted sigh. They were going to make me hit Fritz. And it would be easy: He was already falling back on all the bad habits I'd tried to drill out of him. I waited until he dropped his gloves and reared his arm back for a long slow hook, and I popped him once on the nose with a sharp left jab. I held back, not wanting to hurt him, but he was so small and so surprised he staggered back. The crowd roared. They were loving this.

I gave Fritz a look that said, *Okay? Cut it out!* but he didn't get the message. He flew at me, even more furious now, gloves flailing. He had abandoned all the things I'd taught him by now and was just beating on me wildly. It was easy to duck away from, and the boys booed again when I didn't take another punch.

Fritz grabbed me around the shoulders the way boxers sometimes do when they're tired, locking up my arms. I thought he was just taking a breather, but he'd been trying to get close to my ear. Over the jeers of the crowd, I heard him whisper, *"We can't show weakness. You have to fight me for real."*

I pushed him off me and stared him down. He couldn't be serious. Why couldn't we just spar with each other for a few minutes and be done with it? Why did it have to be for real?

Fritz came at me again, this time remembering some of what I'd taught him. He peppered my face with jabs and I kept up my gloves, but then he got in a hard uppercut to the gut that I couldn't block in time.

I doubled over in pain, and Fritz went for the top of my head. I put my hands up, trying to protect myself, but I was too winded. He was getting in too many good shots. The boys in the crowd were cheering him on and calling me every name you could think of and a few more I'd never heard before.

For two years, I had been the only Irish boy in my entire class at St. Paul's Grammar School in London. And did I mention, the Irish hate the English, and vice versa? Every day at recess I had been dragged behind the gymnasium and thrashed by some hulking lout of an English boy while all the other boys hooted and hollered and laughed at me.

And then, one day, I fought back.

I was like Fritz at first, all desperate anger and flailing arms. I got myself a right proper beatdown that day, for a bully enjoys nothing more than when you try to fight back and fail miserably. But I got up, wiped off the blood, and fought back the next day. And the next. And every day I got a little better, learned a little something more, and one day I gave as good as I got, and the boys stopped dragging me behind the gym for my daily beating.

Because a bully hates nothing more than when you fight back and win.

The constant pounding, the jeering, the familiar queasy feeling I had from the punch to my stomach — it was like being back in the school yard at St. Paul's, taking another beating behind the gymnasium. And I didn't take beatings like that anymore.

I met Fritz's jaw with a vicious uppercut, striking him with all the righteous strength and brutal rage of a boy being bullied. His head snapped, his eyes rolled back in his head, and he toppled forward, hitting the ground at my feet like a sack of potatoes.

MONSTERS

THE BOYS ALL AROUND ME THUNDERED THEIR APPROVAL, their bloodlust ignited, and I stood over Fritz feeling their hunger for more violence. I panted with the deep, furious heave of a prizefighter ready for more. I wanted him to get back up, wanted to hit him again, to punish him for picking a fight with me. I wanted to punch him, kick him, bite him. I wanted to *hurt* Fritz, deeply and permanently.

I blinked, realizing with a start what I was thinking. I shook my head, trying to clear it. How had I slipped into being one of these monsters so easily? How had I forgotten so quickly that I was a human being?

I turned to Horst. "It's over," I said. "I won."

Horst pointed to something behind me. "Not yet!"

I turned just as Fritz connected with a right hook to the side of my head.

The blow staggered me, made my eyes cross, but I didn't go

down. I had enough experience in dirty, behind-the-gymnasium fights to know that when you went down, the fight was over but the beating wasn't.

I kept my feet while Fritz came at me again. There was a dull look in his eyes now, as if my punch had knocked something loose in his brain. I guessed it was his common sense.

Fritz opened himself up again, and I punched him in the nose. Hard. Blood spurted all over his clean, pressed Hitler Youth uniform, and he dropped to his knees, one hand on the ground. The monsters around me howled. They'd finally gotten to see what they came for.

"It's over," I told Fritz. "Stay down."

Fritz got back up.

I punched him in the gut before he could even take a swing at me. Fritz doubled over and crumpled to the ground again.

I felt disgusted at what I'd done. What the Hitler Youth had made me do. I spat at Horst's feet. "We're finished here," I told him. "Call it off."

"No! No, it's not over!" Horst yelled, half laughing with delight. "Get up, Fritz! You're going to fail the test if you don't get up again and fight!"

"No, it's over," I told Fritz. "Stay down. You passed."

Fritz ignored me and pulled himself up again. He staggered for a moment, blood still dripping from his nose, and took another wide, slow swing at me.

I didn't even raise my gloves. I stepped back out of the way and let Fritz's follow-through send him crashing to the ground. He was done.

"For God's sake, Fritz," I begged, *"stay down."*

But Fritz got back up again. And he was going to keep getting back up. I was going to have to finish this the way I'd learned to back on the playground of St. Paul's. I was going to have to put him down so he couldn't get up for more.

I hit him in the face again, but before he could fall I punched him in the stomach. He dropped to his knees and vomited. But he wasn't done, and neither was I. I punched Fritz in the back of the head, sending him down face-first into the puddle of sick. When he moved to get up again, I straddled him and punched him in the back of the head. The laughter and the jeers from the other boys dwindled away to nothing as I punched the back of his head again, and again, and again. I savaged him, fueling each new punch with some new hatred. I hated Hitler for starting this war. I hated the Hitler Youth for their constant bullying. I hated Fritz for making me hit him again. I hated myself for hitting him.

When at last I stopped, Fritz lay motionless on the ground, completely and totally beaten. All around us was utter silence. I looked up, eyes afire, chest heaving, arms tensed for another fight. Horst took a step back in fear. I had managed to scare even the monsters, and when you can scare monsters, you can be sure you've become one yourself.

THE WRONG THING

I SAT GINGERLY IN A CHAIR IN MY DA'S STUDY. I WAS SORE and bruised from the fight, my right eye swollen and black, but it was nothing compared to how I'd left Fritz. They'd had to pick him up and carry him to the nurse's tent. He couldn't even stand up on his own.

Simon walked circles around Da's desk, stretching his legs and testing his ankle. I'd checked and double-checked the door this time to make sure it was locked, but I was still nervous every time Simon was out of his hiding place. He was more and more restless from being cooped up in there all day.

"Did you take the test where you have to jump into the pool?" Simon asked.

"No. Not today. It's tomorrow."

Simon nodded. "Just remember what we've been working on. Distract yourself. Remember that you've been that high before, up on the roof, and survived. And remember why you're doing it. To get close to Fritz and get those plans."

I nodded lamely. Fritz. The boy I'd pummeled within an inch of his life. The boy who hadn't said a word to me the rest of the day, because he couldn't. He'd spent the rest of the afternoon in the nurse's tent.

"How did you like *The Maltese Falcon*?" Simon asked.

I shrugged. "It was okay, I guess."

Simon raised his eyebrows. "*Okay you guess?* It's one of the best books ever written. What about that part where Spade pops Joel Cairo in the nose and takes his gun away from him? I love that bit."

I stared at the floor.

"Michael, what's wrong?"

I sighed. There was no use hiding it from him. He had to know sooner or later.

"It's over," I told Simon.

"What's over?"

"Me and Fritz. The SRD. The jet fighter plans. Everything!" I told him what had happened at the Hitler Youth trials. About me beating Fritz down. Again and again and again.

"It doesn't matter if we both pass the rest of the tests now, and both of us end up in the SRD. *I put him in the hospital*, Simon. He's never going to speak to me again. Not even if we were the last two boys in all of Germany. I wouldn't, if I was him. If my mission was to buddy up to Fritz so I could steal the plans for Projekt 1065, I messed it up royally."

Simon sat on the edge of Da's desk, looking glum. "It does sound bad. But don't be down on yourself, Michael. You did what you had to do—even if doing it meant doing something wrong."

I flipped the edge of the oriental rug up and down with my foot. Doing what you had to do, even though it meant doing something wrong, seemed to be what this war was all about.

"There's always a chance you can make it up to him somehow," Simon said.

I looked at him doubtfully.

Simon got up and paced again. "Before the war, I was stepping out with a beautiful young woman named Mary. We had a wonderful time, Mary and me, going to the cinema, lingering about in cafés, taking moonlit walks along the Thames. But when her parents caught wind of it, they didn't approve. They told her to stop seeing me."

"Because you're English?"

Simon smiled at the latest salvo in our long-running insult contest, but his smile disappeared quickly. Whatever the reason was, it was nothing to laugh about.

"No," he said. "Because I'm Jewish. They may not be carting Jews off to concentration camps in England the way they are in Eastern Europe, but that doesn't mean there isn't still a great deal of anti-Semitism there. Someone won't let you stay in their hotel, or eat in their restaurant. Or marry their daughter." Simon's face tightened. "Mary's parents forbade her marrying me. Said they would never speak to her again if she did. Mary said she didn't care. Said she'd run off with me and get married over the anvil at

Gretna Green if I liked. But her friends and family shunned her, and it was so hard on her. I could see that. It was killing her inside."

"What did you do?"

"What I had to do—and the wrong thing," Simon said quietly. "I broke things off with Mary. Told her we were finished. I admit, it's not like beating another person senseless. But in some ways it was worse. A broken heart is harder to mend than a broken nose. And I ended up breaking two hearts in the bargain. Then the war began, and I was whisked away by the RAF. I haven't seen her since."

Simon looked off into the distance, as if he could see all the way across Europe and the North Sea to England. "Perhaps I should have fought for Mary. Perhaps I should have let her give up everything for me. But I wasn't out to change the world, and neither was she. We were just two kids in love." He sighed. "Who knows? Perhaps after this war, we'll get a second chance. And perhaps you will too, with Fritz."

I hoped he was right, for both of us, but I'm not sure either of us really believed it.

Simon went to his little hideaway and brought back a book. "Here's your next one. Perhaps the greatest English novel of all time."

"Well, that's not saying a lot," I said, trying to lighten things up again with another dig. It was a book called *Kim* by Rudyard Kipling. "Is it another detective novel?"

"No," Simon said, and I groaned. Now that he'd got me hooked, I didn't want to read anything else.

"Don't worry. You'll like it. It's all about an Irish boy who becomes a spy."

NUTTY AS A FRUITCAKE

SIMON'S WORDS ABOUT SECOND CHANCES STAYED WITH me the next morning. Whatever it took, no matter what I had to do, I was going to get Fritz to give me a second chance.

It was another bright, clear morning for the second day of the Hitler Youth initiation tests. More Führer weather. I scanned the waiting crowd of boys for Fritz. Even though he was a head shorter than everyone else, I found him quickly near the front.

He was the one with his head wrapped in white bandages.

There was a red spot on his bandages, near his temple. Fritz's broken nose had been reset and taped. Both his eyes had huge black rings around them, and one of his ears was swollen and bruised.

This was going to be even harder than I thought.

Fritz caught sight of me and pushed through the crowd toward me. People were so afraid of him they moved out of his way. Not because he was so ugly, I realized. Because he'd gotten back up again when they wouldn't have.

The crowd parted for him and watched as he marched over to me, all of them clearly expecting another fight. I braced myself for a punch, ready to take a bloody nose if that's what it took to put us back on the path to, if not friendship, then at least acceptance. Speaking terms.

Fritz threw his arms around me and hugged me instead.

I stood there, stunned, my arms still tensed for a punch. Fritz was . . . *hugging* me?

Fritz let go, and slapped my shoulders as if we were comrades.

"You're—you're not mad?" I asked.

Fritz looked shocked. "Mad? Why would I be mad? We passed our boxing tests! Just one more test to go!"

I shook my head. Frankly, Fritz was starting to scare *me* too. "You're certifiable," I told him. He didn't understand my British idiom. "You're crazy. You don't have any cups in your cabinet."

Fritz just frowned. He still didn't get it.

"I just beat the ever-living snot out of you!" I told him. "You should hate me right now!"

Fritz shook his head. "You just did what I asked you to."

I shook my head again. There was something not right with Fritz. But I wanted those jet fighter plans, and if he was going to forgive me and still be friends, I would accept it. I shook his hand.

"Now," said Fritz, "I'm going to do what you asked *me* to do. I'm going to help you get through the courage test."

ARSCHBOMBE

THE TEST OF COURAGE.

I'd been so upset about blowing my chance to steal the plans for Projekt 1065 that I'd forgotten all about it. The ultimate distraction.

But there was no ignoring it now.

The tower beside the pool was two stories tall and made of crisscrossing wood. A rough ladder went straight from the ground to the top, and boys waited in line on it until there was room for them at the top. From there they plummeted twenty feet to smack down into the icy cold water below.

I stood at the bottom rung of the ladder, hands on the sides, trying to take deep breaths and failing miserably.

"I can do this," I whispered. "I can do this. I can *do* this."

But I couldn't do it. My foot wouldn't lift up off the ground.

"Nope. Can't do it," I said. I let go of the ladder and tried to turn away.

Fritz took me by the shoulders and turned me back around. "Yes, you can, Michael. You have to."

"No. No way," I said. My head spun. My heart raced. I was too worked up. I was getting hysterical.

Fritz dragged me away from the other boys waiting in line. "Michael. *Michael!* Snap out of it. You can't let them see your fear. Do you understand me? If they see you're weak, they'll eat you alive."

I nodded. I knew he was right. If you were tough, people left you alone. If you showed the slightest sign of fear, they would attack. I closed my eyes and tried to control my breathing the way Simon had taught me. I wished he was here right now, but then I remembered why he couldn't be, and why it mattered so much that I overcome my fear of heights and follow Fritz into the SRD.

"You climbed up that ladder in the farmhouse when we were looking for that downed airman," Fritz said, almost reading my thoughts about Simon. It startled me, but I realized there was no way he could know Simon was hidden in my house.

"But even if I get to the top, then I have to — "

"Don't think about that," Fritz said. He guided me back to the bottom rung of the ladder. "One step at a time, right?"

One step at a time. That's what Simon had said too. *Small steps.* I breathed slowly and deeply and lifted my right foot onto the ladder. Then my left. One step at a time. Small steps. Fritz climbed up right behind me, whispering encouragement. We moved up the ladder at a snail's pace, but that was fine by me. I kept my eyes closed and thought about all the insults the English boys had used on me in the school yard in St. Paul's, and all the insults I'd hurled at them in return. They were great motivation—and a great distraction. I made a mental list of a few choice ones I'd use to tease Simon with when I got back.

If I got back.

And then we were at the top. I froze, eyes still closed, but Fritz was there to guide me forward. I took little half steps. I tried to tell myself I wasn't on top of a two-story-tall wooden scaffold, but I was losing the fight. It creaked and swayed. I couldn't do this.

"You're okay," Fritz told me. But I wasn't okay. My stomach seized up, and I felt my breakfast begin to rise in my throat. I dropped down and flattened myself out on the platform. I was never going to move from this spot ever again.

"Come on, Michael," Fritz said. "You just have to do an *Arschbombe*."

He was trying to make me laugh. Trying to lighten the mood. *Arschbombe* meant "butt bomb." It was the German expression for what we called a cannonball—when you wrapped yourself into a tight ball and dove into a pool. Hitting the water with your butt like a bomb.

The mental image distracted me for a few seconds, but then I remembered where I was and why I would never be doing a butt bomb here or anywhere else. I shook my head. I couldn't speak, for fear I would throw up.

"If you don't pass the courage test, you can't be in the SRD," Fritz said. "You can't even be in the regular Hitler Youth!"

I didn't care anymore. I couldn't do it. The Nazis were going to build a jet plane and the Allies were going to lose the war, but I just couldn't do it. I kept my eyes and my lips screwed shut tight.

"Okay," Fritz told me. "It's okay, Michael. You don't have to do it. I'm sorry. I'll help you back down. We're coming back down the ladder!" he called. "Everybody climb back down!"

I heard the cries of annoyance from the boys waiting on the ladder as Fritz helped me stand up. Just getting back down the ladder was going to be impossible.

Fritz guided me, one hand on my arm, the other on my back. "Just keep your eyes shut, Michael," he said. "You don't want to see this."

I nodded, dizzy at the mere *thought* of looking down the ladder. With Fritz's help, I inched back toward it, eyes shut tight.

"I'm sorry, Michael," Fritz told me.

I shook my head. Fritz didn't need to apologize. I was the one who couldn't overcome my fear. He was the one who would become an SRD. Not me. *I* was the one who'd failed.

"No, I mean, I'm *really, really sorry*," Fritz whispered, and he pushed me off the platform.

TAKING THE PLUNGE

I WOULD LIKE TO TELL YOU THAT I FELL BRAVELY. THAT I found a sense of calm, a sense of peace, as I plunged two stories into the pool.

The truth is, I screamed in terror the whole way down. I screamed like a baby who'd dropped his pacifier. I screamed so loud, people probably started running for their cellars in Berlin, thinking I was an air raid siren.

I hit the freezing cold water belly-first, slapping the scream and the rest of my breath right out of me. I swallowed a lungful of water, and would likely have drowned in stunned horror if two Hitler Youth boys hadn't fished me out of the pool. I lay on the ground beside it, soaking wet and sobbing for air. At least the icy water streaming from my plastered hair hid my tears.

I never heard the whoop behind me, or the splash. I never saw him fished out of the pool by the Hitler Youth boys. Somehow, Fritz just appeared above me, bandages dripping with water. He covered me with a blanket.

"You did it!" Fritz said. "You overcame your fear!"

I shook my head. We both knew the truth — I hadn't overcome anything. It had all been Fritz. Without him, I never would have done it. I'd be headed home right now, if not in tears like the weaker boys, then at least as ashamed.

But it didn't matter. I'd taken the plunge, and the judges had seen me do it. I was still in the Hitler Youth. Whether Fritz and I made the SRD was another matter, but at least I was still in the Hitler Youth.

I remembered Fritz hugging me and shaking hands after I'd given him the beatdown of a lifetime. Now it was my turn. I offered him my hand, and he took it, pulling me to my feet.

"Thank you," I told him.

Fritz smiled and shook my hand. We had made it. Together.

Now it was time to get our daggers.

BLOOD AND HONOR

THE HITLER YOUTH INITIATION CEREMONY TOOK PLACE in a massive electrical power plant just outside the city. One wall was filled with switches and dials and little gauges with moving needles. Another was covered with Nazi flags and red, white, and black bunting, over which hung a banner that read WE WERE BORN TO DIE FOR GERMANY. Huge turtlelike generator housings stood in the background like giant sentinels, electrical gods there to watch our induction into the Olympic pantheon. They thrummed with a frantic, hidden energy. The whole place held a sense of power, of modernity, of the future—which I guess is why they held the ceremony there in the first place. The youth were all those things to Nazi Germany—its strength, its break from the past, its hope for the future. Even I was impressed.

I made a mental note of its location so the Allies could bomb it.

An adult Hitler Youth leader—the first one I'd seen all day—stood on a raised metal walkway. Teenagers like Horst ran the smaller troop meetings, but adults from the Hitler Youth administration showed up for bigger missions and medal ceremonies like this one. We listened while he gave a short, boring speech, and then each of us who had passed the initiation tests was called forward to take the Hitler Youth oath.

With a last name starting with *O*, I came in the middle. The Hitler Youth leader told me to put my hand on a folded flag. The flag was called the Blood Banner. Legend had it this banner had been dipped in the blood of the Hitler Youth's greatest martyr, Herbert "Quex" Norkus, who had been killed by a gang of Communist boys back in the days before the Nazis ruled the whole country. I didn't believe it. That Herbert Norkus had been killed, I believed, but I couldn't believe his blood was really on this flag. We were just one small unit of Hitler Youth boys in Berlin. There were hundreds more groups in the city, and thousands more in the rest of the country. If every one of the hundreds of Blood Banners used to initiate new Hitler Youth members all over Nazi Germany had been dipped in the blood of Herbert Norkus, they must have wrung the poor guy out like a sponge before they buried him.

When every last one of us had touched the Blood Banner and recited the oath, the Hitler Youth leader smiled down on us.

"In completing this test, you have fulfilled but a small part of your duty to the Fatherland," he told us. "You do so with pleasure, for millions of your young comrades do the same. You have become a soldier for Adolf Hitler!" He set the needle on a gramophone recording of a trumpet fanfare, and then we sang a couple of Nazi songs. The last one ended with the words "Today Germany listens to us, and tomorrow the whole world," but the boys changed the lyrics, as they always did, to "Today Germany belongs to us, and tomorrow the whole world!" I got a cold shiver, and it wasn't just from my dunk in the pool. If Hitler ever conquered the world, this was how he was going to do it — by turning all of Germany's youth into his willing soldiers.

At last we were all given the thing we had coveted most: the Hitler Youth dagger. We would wear it in a metal sheath on our belt from now on, wherever we went. It was a symbol, a badge of honor that said we had made the cut. The room rang with a collective *shing* as every one of us pulled our daggers from their sheaths at the same time to marvel at them. The handle was black, decorated with a red-and-white checkerboard diamond with a swastika in the middle. A finger guard curled over one side of the hilt. The blade itself was only six inches long, but it was an inch wide, and engraved on it were the words *BLUT UND EHRE!*

Blood and Honor.

"Live faithfully, fight bravely, and die laughing, for you are now officially Hitler Youth!"

The boys cheered, and I raised my fist and pretended to be happy. Nobody cared. As soon as the cheer ended, everyone stampeded over to the bulletin board. It was time to learn which Hitler Youth sections we had been assigned to.

TEARS

MOST OF THE BOYS ENDED UP IN THE GENERAL HITLER Youth. Others had been assigned the sea corps, or the air corps, or the popular motor corps, where you learned to ride motorcycles. I scanned the lists for my name, and there it was: O'Shaunessey, Michael. Streifendienst. The SRD. The junior Gestapo. I'd made it.

I found Fritz on the outskirts of the crowd. My heart sank. There were tears in his bruise-rimmed eyes.

"No—don't tell me you didn't make it!" I said.

Fritz smiled through his tears. "I did. I made it. I can't believe it." He was so happy he was crying. "You made it too, didn't you? I knew you would."

"Why? Just because I conquered the courage test?"

"No. Because you showed them you could be ruthless."

My skin grew cold as I thought again about the beatdown I'd given Fritz in the boxing test.

"You're the reason I got in too," Fritz told me.

"How do you figure that?"

"Because," said Fritz, "you helped me show them that I'm not afraid to die for Germany. Come on. Let's go back to my house and celebrate."

I shook my head as I followed him home. Fritz wasn't as crazy as the rest of the boys.

He was crazier.

We got to Fritz's door. Hidden somewhere behind that door were the secret jet plans that could win the war. Change the world. That door had always been closed to me, but now Fritz was slipping his key in the lock, opening the door, beckoning me inside.

And just like that, I was in. I felt goose bumps as I stepped over the threshold. It was the first step in what was no doubt going to be weeks and weeks of trying to find the hidden plans, but it still gave me a thrill. Now it was time to be a spy.

Fritz lived well. The house had two floors, with rooms on the first floor on each side separated by a long hallway that led back to the kitchen. A staircase ran up one side of the hallway to the second floor. I memorized the layout, began breaking it down into sections to search on different days.

"Come on," Fritz said, running upstairs. "I want to show you something secret."

FRITZ'S SECRET

WAS IT REALLY GOING TO BE THAT EASY? WAS FRITZ GOING to take me right to the rest of the plans for Projekt 1065? He'd brought one of the pages to school to show me before he ever really knew me. Maybe now he was going to show me the rest.

I kept my eyes on the top of the stairs as I followed him, making sure not to look down. Watching us from the railing up above was Fritz's little sister, Lina. Watching *me*, I should say. Her big, wide eyes followed me all the way up the stairs. When I made the turn to follow Fritz back down the hall, I looked over my shoulder. She was still staring at me, expressionless, with those big saucerlike eyes.

"Fritz, your sister really is super creepy."

Fritz shrugged like he was used to it.

I followed Fritz into his room. It was fairly spartan, with a small gray bed, a wooden desk and chair, and an old brown bureau against the wall. Drawings of airplanes were pinned to the wall.

Unfortunately, they weren't the jet fighter plans, just pictures of propeller planes shooting dotted lines at tanks on the ground.

Fritz went straight to his closet and pulled out a small wooden crate from the back. I frowned. If these were the secret jet fighter plans, this was an awfully strange place to hide them. Fritz hesitated, looking at me one last time as though making sure I could be trusted, and lifted the lid.

Inside were stacks of sheet music, like you'd use to play a piano. I frowned. Then Fritz pulled away the music sheets and revealed what was hidden underneath.

Mystery novels. British and American mystery novels.

My disappointment at not finding the plans right away was quickly replaced by my amazement at seeing the treasure trove of books.

"Detective books!" I said. "So that's where you were getting all those English words! And that's why you couldn't burn those books at the bonfire."

Fritz relaxed visibly. "You like them too? I thought you might, being English."

"*Irish*," I said. "But yeah. I just read *The Maltese Falcon*. My friend Si — " I caught myself, horrified that I'd almost said Simon's name. Almost told Fritz that the British Jewish pilot hiding in my house had introduced me to detective novels. But Fritz had just trusted me with his deep dark secret — a secret that could get him and his family shipped off to a concentration camp. Did that mean I could trust him too?

"A friend back in Ireland got me hooked," I said instead. I still couldn't do it. Once you got in the habit of keeping secrets, it was hard to stop.

We spent a happy hour on the floor poring over the novels and talking about our favorite scenes. We promised to swap books from our collections, but of course we had to keep the whole thing hidden from sight.

Fritz's collection *was* a big secret, but not the one I'd been hoping to discover in this house. I still had to find the plans for Projekt 1065. Would I find them in time to get them to the Allies to counter the Nazi jet fighters before they turned the tide of the war? I would just have to come back to Fritz's house as often as I could and find some excuse to go snooping around.

Fritz's mother called him and Lina to dinner, and Fritz walked me to the door. I was pulling on my coat when I saw a messy room through a half-closed doorway off the downstairs hallway. A large desk was covered with stacks of papers and slide rules, and a drafting table stood nearby covered with larger sheets of white paper.

"Oh, that's my dad's study," Fritz said. He stepped inside, and I followed. All over the walls, pinned up around and on top of one another, were a dozen sheets of big blue paper with engineering schematics drawn on them.

"It's the jet plane he's working on," Fritz said. "The one I showed you before." He put his arms out like airplane wings and zoomed around the room.

I blinked stupidly. I think my mouth hung open. There they were, out there for anyone to see, plain as day. The blueprints for Projekt 1065. I wouldn't have to go snooping for them after all. There were too many to memorize all in one day, and Fritz's mother wouldn't exactly let me sit in here and stare at them while they had dinner.

But I would be back tomorrow after school. And the day after that, and the day after that, and the day after that, for as long as it took.

The plans for Projekt 1065 were mine!

KIM'S GAME

EVERY DAY AFTER SCHOOL, I WENT HOME WITH FRITZ, and every day before I left, I popped into his father's study to memorize another part of the blueprints.

"And his father's never there, working on the designs?" Simon asked me one day as I sat with him in his little closet, adding words and numbers I'd memorized to the blueprints we were reconstructing. Ma had brought us big sheets of butcher paper from the store to write on. Some of them still smelled of raw meat.

"His mother and father are always gone," I told Simon. "*Everybody's* mother and father are always gone. There's a joke in Germany about how dad's in the army, mom's in the Nazi Women's League, the son is in the Hitler Youth, and the daughter is in the Bund Deutscher Mädel, and they only get to see each other once a year at the Nazi Party rally."

"Not very funny," Simon said.

"But true," I told him. "In Fritz's case, just substitute his father working for the air force instead of the German army."

"I'm still gobsmacked that you got in there and found the plans, Michael. It's an incredible piece of spycraft." Simon squinted at my terrible handwriting. "What's this word here? *Schwalbe*?"

"It, um — it's the name of the plane."

"But what does it mean?" Simon asked.

I held my breath. I hated to tell him. "It means 'Swallow,'" I told him. "Like the bird. The Messerschmitt Me 262 Swallow." Swallows looked just like swifts.

"Ah," he said, and I could see he was back on that rooftop when he was a boy, caught up in a tornado of birds.

"Have you figured out how you're going to escape from Germany?" I asked, trying to distract him.

"Your mother's been working on it. Apparently, it involves a number of different modes of transportation and many days of travel under cover of darkness. There may even be trench coats and false mustaches. But at the rate you're going with these blueprints, we'll be ready before she is. You've a fine memory, Michael. Have you ever tried to hone it? Practiced getting better at remembering things?"

I shrugged. "I never needed to."

"Your memory can always improve," Simon told me. "Have you gotten to the point in *Kim* where he meets Lurgan Sahib, the gem trader?"

I hadn't. With all my Hitler Youth training and all the evenings spent in here with him transcribing the plans for the Swallow, I hadn't had as much time for reading.

"Slip out to your father's study and bring me a handful of random little things — an eraser, a paper clip, a coin, things like that. As many as you can find."

The door to Da's study was locked, but I still used the little hidden peephole in the shelf to have a look around first. Nothing. I breathed a sigh of relief. The staff weren't supposed to be able to get in, but if one of them was a spy, they could find a way.

When I returned with my modest loot, Simon took the items from me and arranged a few of them unseen underneath his handkerchief.

"This is called Kim's Game, for the game he plays with Lurgan Sahib." Simon pulled the handkerchief away, revealing some of the objects I'd gathered for him. "Study them for as long as you like," he told me. "Pick them up. Handle them if you want. But when you're finished, I'm going to put this handkerchief back over them and have you tell me all about them."

I took a few seconds to memorize what I saw and then I told Simon I was ready. He had me tell him which objects I had seen, and I was able to rattle them off without any problem. "And what did the eraser say on it?" he asked me.

"What?"

"There was a word on the eraser," Simon told me. "Or part of one, at least. Some of it's been rubbed off. What was it?"

I stared at the shelves of books behind Simon, trying to remember, but I couldn't. I'd seen it, but I hadn't really *seen* it.

"Do you understand now?" Simon said. "You remembered what the items were without any problem. But you didn't remember everything about them. But you can. And you will. *If* you train yourself to remember. Do you want to try again?"

I did.

SURRENDER OR DIE

"HEY, REMEMBER THAT KID IN LINE AHEAD OF US AT THE initiation test who got sent home because his parents weren't good Nazis?" Fritz asked me. "There he is."

We stood at the end of a cobblestone street with other members of the SRD, ready, at last, to take on our first assignment for the Hitler Youth Patrol Force. The boy Fritz was talking about stood a little ways off from us wearing a brand-new SRD uniform just like ours.

I frowned. "Didn't he get kicked out?" I said. "What's he doing here, wearing that uniform?"

"His name's Karl. You didn't hear? He made it into the Hitler Youth after all by turning in his parents to the Gestapo."

I shook my head. People were always spying on one another and ratting on each other to the secret police, especially if there was some reason they didn't like them. Someone cuts in front of you in the food ration line? Tell the Gestapo you overheard them complaining about Hitler. Your boss at work gave you a bad review? Tell the Gestapo he's been stealing office supplies. Your neighbor's dog digs holes in your flower bed? Tell the Gestapo your neighbor is hiding a Jew. Turning in your neighbor was the German national pastime.

But to denounce your own *parents*? I shuddered at the thought. If you were denounced for a real reason, it was as good as a death sentence.

"They took them into protective custody," Fritz whispered. Code for being arrested and sent to a concentration camp. "And Karl got an automatic promotion to the SRD."

But of course. If you were a coldhearted weasel who would turn in your parents to get a promotion, you *belonged* in the SRD. I could see that the other SRD boys were giving him plenty of space, but I didn't know if it was out of respect or out of fear.

"SRD, to me!" a man in an SS uniform called, and with a start I realized it was SS-Obersturmführer Trumbauer, the Gestapo man who told the story at dinner about the boy who turned in his parents for harboring a Jew. The SS officer who had almost caught me talking with Simon that night at the embassy. Apparently, ratting out your parents to the Gestapo was a great way to get on his good side. "The rest of you, line up!" he called.

This must be something important for an adult to be here with us, I thought. SS-Obersturmführer Trumbauer caught sight of me. He came over and tapped his riding crop against the silver gorget I wore on my blue SRD uniform.

"Michael O'Shaunessey. I see you chose the SRD," he said, and my skin crawled. "Very impressive."

Beside me, Fritz straightened as though he'd gotten the compliment.

SS-Obersturmführer Trumbauer turned his attention to the other boys, the ones wearing the plain black-and-brown uniforms of the regular Hitler Youth.

"You regular Hitler Youth are here today because we need extra manpower. Members of the Edelweiss Pirates are known to frequent the pool hall at the end of the street, and today, we are going to raid it."

An electric current rippled through the collected boys. Fritz and I turned to stare at each other in surprise. Our first action as SRD, and we were going on a raid! Fritz was excited. I was worried. How could I pretend to be enthusiastic but not hurt anyone?

"I need a volunteer to lead the first wave of the attack," our leader said. He eyed me, but there was no way I was going to be fool enough to be the first person through that door, wearing an SRD uniform, no less! Then, to my surprise, Fritz's hand shot up.

SS-Obersturmführer Trumbauer raised his eyebrows. "And what is your name, young man?"

"Fritz Brendler, sir!"

"Very good, Fritz Brendler," SS-Obersturmführer Trumbauer said. The SS-Obersturmführer gave me a disappointed look and began to separate the regular Hitler Youth boys into small groups and assign them to SRD boys.

I shot Fritz a glance like *Are you crazy?* but he was too excited to notice. I could see that wild look in his eyes again, could see him breathing faster. He barked out an order to his troops, and they ran off down the street toward the pool hall. The rest of us followed on their heels.

"Don't hurt any of them," I told my boys. "We do this the easy way. We're just here to take them into protective custody with as little trouble as possible." Which was a joke, because protective custody meant they were anything but safe. But I didn't want any of the Pirates' blood on my hands, especially when I secretly agreed with them.

We took up positions outside the pool hall. I thought SS-Obersturmführer Trumbauer was going to give us instructions, coordinate things, but Fritz yelled, "This is an SRD raid!" and shot through the front door of the pool hall with all the subtlety of a bazooka. "Surrender or die, Edelweiss pigs!" he screamed.

So much for the easy way. I shook my head and waved my troops inside.

QUEX

THE POOL HALL ERUPTED INTO AN UPROAR OF SHOUTS, screams, shattering glass, and breaking wood. It was almost over by the time I got inside with my troops. The place was a wreck — broken bottles, snapped pool cues, and bloodied patrons everywhere. Fritz was overseeing the arrest of a group of boys and girls just a few years older than we were, while the other Hitler Youth thugs were doing their best to punish the kids they'd captured before turning them over to the Gestapo. I saw one of the Hitler Youth boys using a broken chair leg to beat the limp form of a boy who was slumped unconscious over one of the pool tables, and I grabbed Fritz by the shoulder to show him.

"Horst!" Fritz cried, and I realized to my surprise that's who was doing the beating. Donkey-faced Horst, our former Jungvolk leader. The boy who'd made Fritz fight me during the initiation test.

Fritz marched over to Horst, and Horst froze. There was actually a look of fear in his eyes. Fear of *Fritz*. Everyone had acted weird around Fritz—and me—after our boxing match. But Horst couldn't really be afraid of Fritz, could he? Then I realized—he wasn't afraid of Fritz. He was afraid of the *uniform*. We were SRD now. Junior Gestapo. These uniforms and these silly silver gorgets carried the power to send Horst to a concentration camp.

Horst took a step back and lowered the chair leg.

Fritz stared at him, and I saw a bead of sweat run from Horst's hairline down to his chin.

"Carry on," Fritz said at last.

Horst blinked, and then smiled his horsey smile. He raised the chair leg to hit the prone boy again.

"No, don't!" I said. "Take him into protective custody."

Horst frowned at me, but he obeyed me. I wore an SRD uniform too. He tossed the chair leg away and hauled the boy outside to the waiting truck.

"You're too soft," Fritz told me.

"Fritz, we don't even know if that boy is a Pirate or not!"

"He's in a pool hall smoking cigarettes and listening to American music during the day instead of participating in the Hitler Youth. That's crime enough."

I wanted to remind him that he had a box of American books at home, but SS-Obersturmführer Trumbauer appeared beside us, and I clammed up.

"You were so quick to volunteer," he told Fritz, "and so quick into the fray. We should call you Quex." *Quex* was shorthand for the German word for "quicksilver." To call someone Quex meant they were quick. But there was much more to the nickname than just speed. That was the nickname of Herbert Norkus — the boy whose blood was supposedly soaked into the Blood Banner we'd taken our oath on. To call Fritz "Quex" was like comparing him to one of the most famous Hitler Youth ever, a fact that wasn't lost on Fritz. I don't know how it was possible, but Fritz looked about three inches taller right then.

"I'm putting together a special team, Brendler," SS-Obersturmführer Trumbauer told Fritz. "And I think you would be a perfect fit. Report to me tomorrow instead of going to your regular SRD duties."

"Yes, sir! Heil Hitler!" Fritz cried, giving Trumbauer an enthusiastic Nazi salute. I fought hard not to show my disgust.

"Nice job, Quex!" the SRD boys told Fritz as they filed out.

"Surrender or die!"

"Good one, Quex."

"Did you hear that?" Fritz asked me as we walked out together. "The SS-Obersturmführer wants me for a special team! He called me Quex!"

"Yeah, um, Fritz? Didn't Herbert Norkus die young?" I reminded him.

"He died a *hero*," Fritz said, missing my point entirely.

KUDDELMUDDEL

THE EDELWEISS PIRATES WERE QUIET FOR THE NEXT FEW days. But one morning as I walked to school I saw that more graffitied edelweiss had bloomed among the red, white, and black Nazi flags on the bombed-out walls of Berlin.

The Hitler Youth had won a battle against the Edelweiss Pirates, but the war against them wasn't over. Neither was the real war. It was late February, the hardest part of the winter, and Germany was now fighting on three fronts—east, west, and south—and none was going well. Rationing was tight, new winter clothes were scarce, and four inches of snow had fallen on the city overnight. It was like even nature was against the Nazis. The Führer weather had definitely run out.

But no one said so, of course. No one said much of anything. They kept their collars turned up and their hats down and their scarves wrapped tight around their faces, hiding from each other as they passed on the street.

But people still knew to cross the street before they walked past me. It was the uniform. No one wanted to be caught doing the wrong thing, and no one was ever really sure what the wrong thing might be.

I climbed the steps to Fritz's house and knocked on the door, stamping my feet to try to keep them warm. The door finally opened, but it wasn't Fritz. It was his little sister, Lina. She was dressed in her BDM uniform and ready for school.

"Is Fritz home?" I asked.

Lina just stared at me.

"Can I come in? It's cold out here."

Lina closed the door on me.

My breath came out in a gray cloud as I huffed. For days now, I hadn't been able to catch Fritz at home, which meant I'd gone days without a glimpse at the blueprints for Projekt 1065. All I needed was a few more minutes with the last page, and I'd have them all! But whatever special SRD team Trumbauer had put Fritz on was eating up all his free time.

The door opened again, and Lina was dressed in her winter coat and carrying her rucksack.

"No Fritz?" I asked.

Lina shut the door behind her and locked it, then turned and waited.

"Do you ever speak?" I asked her.

Lina just stared at me.

I threw up my hands. "Okay. Let's go," I told her. "It's too cold to talk anyway."

We walked to school in silence. I dropped Lina off at her classroom and went to mine. Fritz wasn't there, either. Where was he? What was he up to?

I reached into my rucksack and took out the essay we'd been assigned the day before — "Ten Ways to Have Fun Doing More with Less." I walked over and put it in the growing stack on Herr Professor Doktor Major Melcher's desk.

His desk was what the Germans would call a *Kuddelmuddel*. It means "a mess." Chaos. Disorganization. Herr Professor Doktor Major Melcher's desk looked as if he'd taken his top drawer and overturned it on the surface. It was covered in paper clips and pencils and rubber bands and scribbled notes.

The items reminded me of the game I'd been playing with Simon every night, Kim's Game. I took a moment before Herr Professor Doktor Major Melcher got there to practice it again. I studied each item on the desk in turn, trying to memorize everything about it. Not just what was there, but what position it was in, what its meaning might be (the pencils were all chewed at the top — Herr Professor Doktor Major Melcher was nervous about something), and if anything was written on them.

One of the little slips of paper buried in the *Kuddelmuddel* on his desk said, "REGRET TO INFORM YOU YOUR s — " but I couldn't read the rest. I gave a German Look around to see if anybody was watching. They weren't.

I pulled the paper out and read it, and all at once I understood why Herr Professor Doktor Major Melcher had stopped hiding how much he hated the Nazis.

THE WOLF PACK

THE PAPER ON MELCHER'S DESK WAS A TELEGRAM
from the Nazi High Command. It was dated several weeks
ago—just after the German defeat at Stalingrad. Under Herr
Professor Doktor Major Melcher's name and home address, it
said:

REGRET TO INFORM YOU YOUR SON UNTEROFFIZIER JÜRGEN
MELCHER KILLED IN GLORIOUS SERVICE TO FATHERLAND ON
1ST FEBRUARY DURING STRATEGIC WITHDRAWAL OF FORCES
FROM STALINGRAD. HEIL HITLER.

So that explained it. Why Herr Professor Doktor Major Melcher
had been so angry these past weeks. Why he'd been letting his
doubts about Hitler and the war creep into his lessons. His son
had died at Stalingrad. "Strategic withdrawal." Ha. Just like
"protective custody," "strategic withdrawal" was code. It meant

"we ran away like cowards." Sergeant Jürgen Melcher had died running from the Russians with the Sixth Army the day before the rest of his comrades just gave up and surrendered.

Fritz finally showed up for class, talking and laughing with another SRD boy named Max.

I called Fritz over. "Take a look. I found something that explains why Herr Professor Doktor Major Melcher has been so touchy lately."

"He's been touchy because he's a doddering old man who serves no purpose to the war effort," Fritz said.

I recoiled a bit from the strength of Fritz's reaction. He'd never been so hateful before.

"We have no use for these clever monks in their quiet cells," Max said, spouting overblown propaganda from our weekly meetings. "The future will not be won with essays and tests. It will be won with fists and steel!"

Fritz nodded in sour agreement.

"No, listen," I tried to tell them, but Herr Professor Doktor Major Melcher walked in just then. I dropped the telegram and hurried away to my desk.

"Sit down and shut up, you brats," Melcher said.

Fritz slid into the seat beside mine. Ever since we'd put on the SRD uniforms, no one had tried to make him sit elsewhere. He sat ramrod straight, eyes forward. He didn't seem to want to talk to me at all these days, and less than a month ago, he'd been following me around like a puppy.

"Fritz, what have you been up to these past few days?" I whispered. "You're never at home in the mornings or after school, and you don't come to the Hitler Youth meetings anymore. What is this special team Trumbauer put you on?"

"It's a . . . a science team," Fritz said.

In the desk behind Fritz, Max snickered like he was in on the joke. And "science team" *had* to be a joke. The only "science" Hitler Youth ever learned was how to tell a Jew from an Aryan and how to calculate the money wasted taking care of mentally handicapped people. I waited for Fritz to tell me the truth, but that appeared to be all he was going to say about it. I smoldered. What was up with Fritz all of a sudden? It was as though we suddenly weren't friends anymore.

Herr Professor Doktor Major Melcher walked up and down the rows of desks, handing back graded papers. He put one on Fritz's desk.

Fritz reached down slowly and flicked it away. The paper fluttered off his desk and landed on the floor at Herr Professor Doktor Major Melcher's feet.

"Pick that up at once!" Melcher said.

"No," said Fritz. "*You* pick it up."

The room got deathly quiet, and a cold pit opened up in my stomach. Fritz didn't know what had happened to Melcher's son. He was going to push him too far.

Herr Professor Doktor Major Melcher's face reddened. "I will do no such thing! Pick that paper up at once, young man, or I will mark this incident down in your Nazi Party record book!"

Fritz slowly got up from his desk. The entire room was silent, watching.

"No," Fritz said again. His voice was cool. Collected. The direct opposite of Herr Professor Doktor Major Melcher's nervous spluttering. "I told *you* once to pick it up," Fritz said. "I won't tell you again."

I couldn't believe Fritz. What was he doing? Herr Professor Doktor Major Melcher shook like he was about to explode. He raised a hand to give Fritz a sharp blow with the back of his hand, but suddenly Max stood up behind Fritz. Then the two other SRD boys in the room. The junior Gestapo, all staring with cold, dead eyes at Herr Professor Doktor Major Melcher. Melcher stood frozen, hand still raised, eyes bulging in a mix of indignation and horror. Fritz glanced at me. I was the only SRD boy not standing, not challenging Melcher.

I stood up. I had to. I couldn't sit while the other SRD boys stood. Otherwise I ran the risk of blowing my cover.

Herr Professor Doktor Major Melcher's bushy eyebrows knitted together in anger and he opened his mouth to say something, but what we heard instead was the howl of the air raid siren. The Americans were at it again. We had to get to the shelters.

Fritz stepped away from his desk, deliberately walking, not running, past Herr Professor Doktor Major Melcher to the door. The other Hitler Youth boys did the same, filing past him in a silent procession of unexpressed violence. Melcher stood rooted to the spot, looking suddenly much more frail and old than his actual years.

I let out the breath I didn't know I'd been holding and ran to my air raid station. Whatever it was Fritz was doing before and after school for the SRD with Max, it was changing him. He was harder now. Colder. Meaner. He never would have talked back to Herr Professor Doktor Major Melcher like that before. And he never would have lied to me.

And if Fritz wasn't going to tell me the truth about what he was doing for SS-Obersturmführer Trumbauer, I was just going to have to find out on my own.

ONE DAY

"YOU HAVEN'T BEEN ABLE TO GET BACK INTO FRITZ'S house?" Ma asked.

We all sat together later that night in Da's study—me, my parents, and Simon. The servants had been sent home for the night, but even so, the study door was locked and the radio was on in the background in case anyone outside stopped to listen in. It was playing a speech by Joseph Goebbels, the Nazi propaganda minister.

"No," I said wearily. I had gotten up before dawn, been to school, worked through two air raids, gone on SRD patrol, and come home after dark. I was beat. "He's been put on some special team by SS-Obersturmführer Trumbauer. They're up to something. I just don't know what." I told them all about Fritz's absences and his reference to the "science team."

"I agree it's not a science team," Da said. "Definitely suspicious."

"They're obviously up to no good," Simon said. "London will be very interested to hear all about it, I'm sure, whatever it is. Something to keep investigating after I'm gone."

"After you're gone?" I said. The plan had always been to get Simon out of Berlin, back to England. But the way he'd said it, like he already knew he was leaving, and soon . . . I looked back and forth between him and my mother.

"It's all set, Michael," Ma said. "He leaves tomorrow night."

"Tomorrow night?"

My heart leaped into my throat. For as hard as I'd worked to steal jet fighter plans and send them back to England with Simon, I realized suddenly that I didn't really want him to go.

"But—Projekt 1065. The jet fighter plans. We're not finished," I said lamely, looking for any excuse I could to keep him here. Yes, I had painstakingly memorized and redrawn eleven pages of schematics with Simon over the last couple of weeks, but there was still one page left to memorize. One page that had no pictures, but was full of math—and math was to engineers what violence was to the Nazis. It was their lifeblood. What made everything possible. We *needed* that last page.

Simon smiled regretfully. "I suppose if you can't set eyes on it by tomorrow night, we'll have to do without and hope the rest is enough for the RAF's engineers to understand. But I've just got to get home, Michael."

I saw at once how selfish I was being. How much Simon hated being cooped up in that little closet all day. Never getting outside.

Never seeing the sun. Away from his friends and family. Away from Mary. Constantly in danger of being discovered and killed. *Or worse.*

Simon was leaving tomorrow night, whether I liked it or not.

"And none too soon," Ma said. "We've got something else to worry about."

"A coded message we intercepted," Da said. "About an assassination the Nazis are planning."

"What? When? Against whom?" Simon asked.

"We don't know," said Ma. "We only just saw a reference to it. I've asked the wife of the Gestapo chief out to lunch tomorrow, hoping to pick something up from her. She likes to talk when she's had a few glasses of wine."

"And I'm meeting for an interview tomorrow with a reporter I know from the *Völkischer Beobachter*, the Nazi newspaper," Da said. "Sometimes I'm able to exchange information with him. Off the record, of course."

"But the long and the short of it, Michael, is that we need Simon to move on so *we* can move on," Ma said. "We've got to get back to the mission. Find out whatever we can about this assassination and try to warn London before it happens."

I nodded. I had one day to get inside Fritz's house and see the last page of Projekt 1065. One day before Simon was gone from Berlin for good.

THE OLD RELIC

I WENT STRAIGHT TO FRITZ'S HOUSE EARLY THE NEXT morning, hoping to catch him before he left for whatever the "science team" was, but he was already gone. I had to get inside that house before the end of the day! Silent, bug-eyed Lina was there, of course, and with a sigh I walked her to school again.

I found Fritz after I'd dropped his sister off at her classroom. He stood outside our school building, huddled together with Max and a dozen more SRD boys — some of whom weren't even in our class. I felt my breathing quicken. Something was up.

"Michael! There you are," Fritz said. "Where have you been?"

"Walking your sister to school," I said, a little testily. "Where have *you* been?"

"Rounding up the boys," Fritz said, indicating the other SRD boys with a nod. His eyes were alive with mischief, the way they had been before the raid on the Edelweiss Pirates. "We're going to get rid of the old relic once and for all."

"What old relic?"

"Melcher!" Fritz said. "I've brought the whole SRD in on it."

Was this what Fritz and Max had been disappearing to work on all this time? Some plan to get rid of Herr Professor Doktor Major Melcher?

"Listen, Melcher's been a jerk lately, but he's been through a lot," I told them. "His son died at Stalingrad. I saw the telegram."

"*Everybody* lost somebody at Stalingrad," Fritz said.

"Really?" I said, suddenly angry. "Did *you*?" I knew he hadn't. "Did you, Max?"

"It's the ultimate honor to die for the Führer," Max said. More bleeding propaganda. It was all that ever came out of Max's mouth.

Fritz nodded. "The old man should be proud his son died for Hitler. Not go soft. He's a defeatist. Germany can't win with people like him around."

I huffed. This was stupid. "Melcher is a patriot. Herr Professor Doktor *Major* Melcher, remember? He fought for Germany in the Great War!"

"The *old* Germany," Fritz said. He wouldn't be swayed. "Is he in there?" he asked.

"Yes, Quex," one of the boys said. Fritz's new nickname had caught on fast.

"Then let's go!"

Fritz charged inside. I didn't even have time to warn Herr Professor Doktor Major Melcher. He was sitting at his desk, his head in his hands, when the SRD blitzed in like the Third Army invading Poland.

"Seize him!" Fritz ordered, and half a dozen boys jumped the old man. They pulled at his coat, his shirt, his tie, ripping his clothes and sending him crashing to the ground. Melcher cried out, but that only seemed to energize them more. They were like wild dogs ripping and tearing at a piece of raw meat. They kicked him and punched him and tried to pull him apart by the arms and legs.

"Don't hurt him!" I cried, but no one was listening to me. I felt the same urge to defend my teacher that I'd felt for Fritz all those weeks ago during the book burning. I tried to fight my way into the wolf pack, but there were too many of them. And it wasn't even all of them. The rest of the boys overturned desks, threw papers in the air, smashed the windows. The other students stood at the edges of the room and cheered them on. I backed away against the doorjamb, horrified by the abrupt violence. The animal cruelty.

There was nothing I could do. Not by myself. But that didn't mean I couldn't call for help. I ran outside to a police box and called in an emergency. It was all I could do. The city police weren't the Gestapo. They could stop this madness. Arrest the boys for attacking Melcher and destroying the school. But only if they got here in time.

If they didn't, the SRD boys were going to kill him.

A WEE IRON COFFIN

TWO POLICE OFFICERS ARRIVED BY CAR JUST AS THE
boys were dragging Herr Professor Doktor Major Melcher out of
the school. I sagged with relief. I'd saved him!

But when the police saw the attackers were SRD boys, they
pulled up short.

"This man is a defeatist!" Fritz announced to the police officers. "We're taking him to the Gestapo!"

The police backed off and let the boys drag Melcher away down
the street. I couldn't believe what I was seeing. The police were
adults! Didn't they see what was happening here? Wasn't somebody going to make the children behave?

Not today. The police were scared. You could see it in the looks
they gave each other. Nervous glances that said, *If we do or say
anything, they'll come for us next*. Idiots! Didn't anybody realize
this was how Nazi Germany had gotten to be this way in the first
place?

I was about to say something, stand up to the SRD bullies, tell the police about Melcher's son, tell them how Fritz and the other boys were wrong. Break this spell of silence. But then I caught myself. If I said something, I might save Melcher's life. But I would ruin everything else Simon and my parents and I had worked for. All our plans to smuggle Simon out with the blueprints. Even if Fritz didn't get me kicked out of the SRD, he would never invite me inside his house ever again. I would never get the last page of the jet plans. Germany would win the war. Crush the Allies. Conquer the world. And what would I have done besides save Herr Professor Doktor Major Melcher's life?

Again I saw myself four years ago, on the Night of Broken Glass. But now I saw it through new eyes — the eyes of my parents. Saw the awful trade: one man's life against the fate of the entire world. My heart ached, as if it were slowly eating me up from inside.

Sometimes we have to sacrifice good people to win a war, Simon had told me. *Sometimes you do what you have to do, even if doing it means doing something wrong.*

Melcher's watery, desperate eyes found mine, and in that moment, I knew. I knew that deep down he really hated the Nazis, and that he'd been faking his loyalty to them all this time.

And that he knew I had been too.

Melcher's eyes begged me to say something. To speak up for him. To save him.

Instead, I said nothing. I locked my heart away in a wee iron coffin and swallowed the key. It burned going down and tears stung my eyes, but still I said nothing.

Herr Professor Doktor Major Melcher closed his eyes and wept. But he didn't give me away. He understood. Because to his own shame, he'd been silent too.

I followed the boys to Gestapo headquarters, where they dumped the broken, blubbering body of Herr Professor Doktor Major Melcher on the floor in front of the SS officer on duty.

"This man has forsaken the Führer and is undermining our will to fight," Fritz told him. How Fritz, the youngest and smallest of them, had become the de facto leader of the group, I didn't know.

"A concentration camp is too good for him!" Max cried.

"Put a rifle in his hands and send him to the eastern front," Fritz said. "Maybe then he'll appreciate what he did to sabotage support for our soldiers while he was safe and warm back in Berlin."

There were indignant nods of agreement all around.

The SS officer called for men to come and take Herr Professor Doktor Major Melcher away. "We'll take care of him," the SS man said. My heart banged against the door of the little box where I'd locked it away, but I didn't let it out. Nobody deserved what was about to happen to Melcher, but I couldn't stop it. Not if I wanted to get the jet plans. But I died inside a little too.

"You won't be needing a teacher any longer anyhow," the SS officer said, and suddenly he had everyone's attention. "You won't have time for it. All Luftwaffe ground specialists have been redeployed to active fighting, which means more duties will fall to the Hitler Youth here at home. From now on, you boys will be manning the antiaircraft guns during air raids."

ONE LAST TIME

WE HAD OUR FIRST TRAINING ON THE GIANT ANTIAIR-craft guns that day, on a training field just outside the city. School was officially out for every boy old enough to fight. Forever.

I should have been happy about that — it had to mean the Nazis were losing, desperate. Or I should have been excited, like the rest of the boys, to get to fire the enormous, house-size gun. But all I could think about was the jet fighter plans in Fritz's house, and the clock ticking away the hours and minutes until Simon escaped from Berlin. I *had* to get into Fritz's house by the end of the day.

I kept trying to catch Fritz, to casually mention getting together this afternoon at his house to read detective novels, but I never had the chance. He had a new group of friends now, and he didn't have time for me. When they loaded us up to take us back to the city at the end of the day, I couldn't even get on the same truck as Fritz. There wasn't any room around him.

I lost Fritz in the *Kuddelmuddel* of boys climbing out of trucks. Had he gone straight to whatever the "science team" was? Or had that special team really been about Melcher? Was it over? Had Fritz gone home? I huffed, my breath spewing like a dragon as I sprinted the ten blocks to his house.

Lina answered the door, her big eyes staring at me.

"Is — is Fritz home?" I said, panting from the run.

Lina stared at me.

"*Lina*, is Fritz home?"

Lina shook her head. She started to shut the door, but I was done waiting around for Fritz. I didn't have time, I stuck my foot in the door.

"Can I come in and wait for him?" I asked Lina. She was probably the only one home.

Lina stared at me for a few more seconds, then opened the door to me. *Yes.* I almost cried for joy. *I was in.* A quick glance at the blueprints one last time, and then I never had to come here again.

Lina closed the door behind me, and I waited in the hall.

Lina stood watching me.

"You can go do whatever it was you were doing," I told her.

She kept staring at me, like she always did.

"Seriously, go. Get," I told her, as if she was some annoying puppy. At last she turned and went upstairs.

I shook my head as I stepped inside Fritz's father's study.

Crazy girl, I thought, and then I suddenly pulled up short, my breath catching in my throat.

All the blueprints were gone from the walls.

LUCKY MUSHROOM

NO. NO NO NO NO NO! I WAS SO CLOSE TO BEING FINISHED! I just needed a few more minutes with the last page of the blueprints. I spun in the office, hoping Fritz's father had just taken them down and they were still stacked up somewhere. But the place was as much of a *Kuddelmuddel* as Herr Professor Doktor Major Melcher's desk. I didn't see them anywhere. My heart burst out of that wee iron coffin and thumped against my chest as I clawed through the piles of papers around the room.

Up until now, I'd been a *Glückspilz*, a weird German expression that meant "lucky mushroom." (Which I guess is no weirder than saying I was a lucky duck. But it still sounded funny.) I'd met the one kid in all of Berlin who could give me access to top secret Nazi jet fighter plans, and he and I had become friends, helping each other pass our Hitler Youth tests and reading forbidden detective novels together while day by day I snuck secret looks at the blueprints for Projekt 1065. But suddenly I'd gone from being a *Glückspilz* to a *Pechvogel* — a "bad luck bird."

I kept digging through the stacks of papers in Fritz's father's office, worried that any moment I was going to hear the front door open and Fritz or his father or his mother would catch me.

Stop, I told myself. *Calm down. What would Simon do?* I suddenly remembered Kim's Game. Fritz's father's office was one giant Kim's Game, one I'd been looking at for weeks now. The key wasn't to dig through all the stacks of paper I'd seen there before. I needed to see what was different now. What was new. I turned around slowly, scanning every inch of the room. And that's when I saw it. A thick accordion folder tied up with string by the door, addressed to be mailed. I snatched it up and took it to Fritz's father's desk. I held my breath as I untied the string. Opened it. Lifted the flap. Saw folded blue papers peeking back at me from inside.

Yes! I almost jumped and yelled for joy. From lucky mushroom to bad luck bird and back again! I was tempted to run away with the packet, take the whole thing to Simon and send him on his way with it. But that was greedy, and foolish. I had already transcribed almost all the plans. Stealing the whole packet now was pointless, and would just let Fritz's father know that their plans had been compromised. I had to memorize the last page and put everything back exactly how I'd found it.

I flipped through the blueprints, found the one I needed, and unfolded it on the desk. I was about to start memorizing the math on it when I got that weird feeling you get when you know someone's watching you.

I looked up and saw Lina in the doorway, staring right at me.

HAVING BABIES
FOR HITLER

MY HEART CAUGHT IN MY THROAT. I WAS BUSTED. *Glückspilz* to *Pechvogel* to *Glückspilz* to *Pechvogel*.

There was no telling how long Lina had been standing there staring at me. But long enough, I was sure, to have seen me open up one of her father's personal packages and pull out a blueprint. Should I grab the last page and run? Try to bluff my way out of it, leave, and hope she never told her parents or brother?

But if Fritz's father was about to mail the plans away, this was my last chance to see them—and maybe the last chance the Allies had to intercept them before they were used to build a working jet fighter that would change the world forever. I didn't know what to do. I was as paralyzed as if I was standing on top of that ladder over the pool again.

"You and I can get married," Lina said.

My mouth hung open. On the list of things I thought Lina might say to me in that moment, "You and I can get married" was right below "I'm an alien from outer space." I was thirteen years old. She was ten years old. Why in the world would either of us be thinking about getting *married*?

"Um . . . okay," I said.

"At first I thought you might not be Aryan, and then we couldn't get married," Lina said. It was more words than she had spoken to me in the entire month I'd known her. "But I asked at the BDM meeting. English is Aryan too. Not as good as Nordic, but okay."

"I'm *Irish*," I told her.

She nodded as though there wasn't any difference. "After I graduate from the BDM and you graduate from the Hitler Youth, we can get married and have lots of babies for Hitler."

"*Whoa, whoa, whoa,*" I told her. I wasn't having lots of babies with anybody or *for* anybody, especially not Hitler. This girl had our whole future planned out, and we'd barely had a single conversation! I was about to argue with her, but I realized it didn't really matter. All that mattered was getting out of here with the plans.

"Listen, it sounds like you've got it all figured out," I told her. "But like you said, we can't do anything until we graduate from the Hitler Youth and the Bund Deutscher Mädel, and then I'll be in the army, and you'll be in the Nazi Women's League or working in a factory somewhere — "

"We can get married in between," Lina said. "Then I can send cigarettes and treats to you at the front lines and you can write me letters back telling me how much you miss me."

I gawked at her. She really had thought this all out.

"Right. Okay. Good plan," I said. I had to get this over with. "So we'll just . . . we'll just wait until we graduate, and then we'll get married and start having lots of babies for Hitler."

"Okay," she said, and she turned and left the room.

I slumped down onto the desk, my face turning red with embarrassment. Lina had been weird all this time because she had a *crush* on me.

This was the last thing I needed to deal with right now.

But maybe it *was* just what I needed. As long as Lina thought we were getting married, she wouldn't be telling on me to her family.

I memorized the last page, put the plans back where I'd found them, and hurried out of the house. I wanted to get out of there before Lina came back to tell me where we were going on our honeymoon.

THE GAME

I DIDN'T TELL SIMON ABOUT MY CONVERSATION WITH Lina. We wouldn't have gotten any work done, he'd be laughing so hard. Instead, we spent what time he had left drawing up the last page of the jet fighter plans from my memory.

And then we were done. There was no more reason for Simon to stay.

"This is a swell piece of work, Michael," Simon told me, apparently not feeling any of the ache I was feeling at his imminent departure. He bundled up the pages we had worked on together and tied a leather string around them. "It's an incredible coup. I came to take pictures, and I'll be going back with full-blown schematics. They'll be waiting to pin a medal on you when you get back to England."

Sad as I was, I liked the thought of that. Michael O'Shaunessey, decorated Irish spy!

My mother and father joined us.

"I've set the staff to cleaning the silverware," Ma whispered, locking the door to Da's study behind her. "That should keep them busy for a time."

"They have to be suspicious of all our locked-door family meetings," Da said.

"It'll all be over tonight," Ma said. "It's all arranged," she told Simon. She spread a map out on Da's desk. "When the nightly air raid comes — and it will, as sure as eggs is eggs — you'll wait until three forty-five in the morning and then make your way to this alleyway, here, where Michael will meet you."

"I will?" I asked. It was the first I'd heard of it.

Ma nodded. "Your da and I can't leave the air raid shelter, or there'd be questions. You know every inch of this city, Michael, and Simon doesn't. Not only that, your SRD uniform will make most people look the other way. Since you'll already be out and about on your patrols, it shouldn't be any problem for you to lead him through the city to his next contact."

"But I won't be on patrol tonight," I told them. "The SRD will be manning the antiaircraft guns."

It was as if I'd dropped a bomb all my own in my father's study. Ma's mouth opened, but nothing came out. Da's face went ashy white.

"Good lord, Michael," Simon whispered. "You can't be serious. That's a death sentence, and you're — *you're thirteen-year-old boys.*"

I didn't know what to say. I didn't have any choice in the matter. None of us did.

"Do you think you can still get away?" Ma finally asked. "It wouldn't be for all night. Just long enough to get Simon to Friedrichstrasse."

"I—I think so. Sure. Yes," I said. It made sense that Simon's escape would take place during an air raid. Almost everybody else would be hiding underground, or have other things to worry about.

"I'm sorry, but are we just going to gloss over the fact that Michael is now a *target* for Allied bombers?" Da asked, looking upset.

"We can't worry about that right now," Ma said.

"*Can't worry about that right now?*" Da said. "Our son might as well be on the front lines, fighting for Hitler. It's become too dangerous here, for him and for us. Someone else without a family can take my place as ambassador."

I started to protest that I could handle it, but Da cut me off with a stern shake of his head.

"No. It's time for us to go back to Dublin."

"We have to get Simon out of Berlin first," Ma said, ending the argument for the moment. She pointed to the map. "Michael, you'll take him here, to this corner on Friedrichstrasse. That's where you'll hand Simon off to one of my agents. You're to tell the agent, 'This air raid sounds like the finale to a Wagner opera,' to which he will respond, 'I prefer Beethoven's symphonies, myself.' That's how you will know he's our man. If he doesn't give you the correct pass phrase, move on."

I nodded, practicing the words in my head.

"Where will he take Simon?" I asked.

"It's best you not know that," Ma said. "The man you're to meet will be the first of my network to ferry him out of the country, but by no means the last. Just do your part, and the network will see to the rest. God willing, Simon will be back in London by St. Patrick's Day."

"Where I'll raise a pint of Guinness and sing the Irish national anthem in your honor," Simon told us with a wry smile. "Now, where are you on this assassination business? Any clue to who they're targeting?"

"We're narrowing it down to a list of targets—an American businessman visiting Portugal, a French Resistance fighter in Algiers, a member of the Danish monarchy," Ma said. "But it's all speculation at this point. We haven't got a solid shred of evidence one way or another. But Davin and I will deal with that." She nodded at my father, and then looked back at Simon. "The first order of business is getting you out of here."

"And then," Da said firmly, "we will talk about how we get *ourselves* out of here."

X MARKS THE SPOT

AIR RAID SIRENS SCREAMED. BERLINERS RAN FOR BOMB shelters. Giant searchlights clicked on, buzzing as they warmed up. From high in the cloudy night sky, we could hear the low, steady, ominous drone of British airplanes growing closer.

And I, along with my SRD troop, stood right in the middle of the street, waiting to shoot them down with an antiaircraft gun.

The antiaircraft guns weren't just "guns." They were *cannons*. The barrel of the gun was a long, thin shiny silver proboscis like a mosquito's nose, sticking out of a stocky jumble of gray hydraulic pistons and levers and gears that could swivel the cannon in any direction and any elevation. The giant mosquito stood on four thin legs that stretched out like an *X* on the ground beneath it — a perfect target for the bombers overhead.

X marks the spot.

And if the *X* wasn't enough, the bombers could target the giant searchlights not three meters from each antiaircraft emplacement. We were just begging to be bombed.

The other boys didn't see it that way. Or if they did, they hid it well. Excitement passed through our little group of a dozen boys like static electricity. They were going to be firing real guns, in a real war situation! At last, no more childish assignments checking IDs or raiding pool halls or tattling on unenthusiastic Hitler Youth. We were going to be doing real fighting.

The *thooms* of exploding British bombs began, and we heard the *pok-pok-pok* of the AA guns beginning to fire on the far side of the city. Our searchlight swept the sky. Black dots of death rained down, and white streaks of death shot up. The once-a-night aerial fistfight between Great Britain and Nazi Germany.

I was one of the boys assigned to run the artillery shells from the storage crate to the gun. Ours was one of the "88s," the cannons that shot enormous 88mm shells that looked like bullets made for a giant's rifle. The shells were two feet long and weighed more than twenty pounds each. The other boys and I had to constantly run back and forth, each of us carrying one in our arms, and hand them off to the boys who fed them into the metal insect's butt. More boys ran the radar machine that helped find the planes in the cloudy skies, and others worked the controls to aim the gun and fire. Fritz and Max were on the team that fired.

The booming orange eruptions of flame grew near. A building a few blocks from us exploded, scattering brick and rubble into the street like a farmer casting seeds. We flinched, and I felt a little of the electric excitement fade away, replaced by fear. But then Fritz was screaming "Fire!" and our AA gun recoiled with the force of a colossal jackhammer, cracking the pavement as it sent its first shell hurtling into the sky. We all stood and watched, even though we'd been trained to reload and fire, reload and fire. In what seemed like slow motion, the tracer round arced high into the clouds and detonated with a distant *poom* between the hundreds of bomber planes flying by. We hadn't hit a thing.

"Reload! Reload!" Fritz cried, and we fell back onto the routine we'd been trained for. Grab a shell from the crate, haul it to the gun, load it, aim it, shoot it. Grab a shell from the crate, haul it to the gun, load it, aim it, shoot it. The routine had been easy to follow in the training session in broad daylight, with no planes droning overhead, no bombs whistling as they fell on you.

A building across the street detonated suddenly, showering us with wooden splinters and bits of masonry. I ducked and put a hand to my helmet to keep it in place as a piece of metal shrapnel pinged off it. The explosion was so loud my ears rang, and I saw instead of heard Fritz calling for another round. All about us the air was filled with dark black smoke that smelled like gunpowder and ash.

I glanced at my watch. 3:15. I had to keep an eye on the time. I had to be at the rendezvous at exactly 3:45 to take Simon across the city to the next agent in Ma's network.

I hefted another cartridge and turned to take it to the gun when the other boys erupted in a cheer. I blinked and looked up at the strobing night sky. A bomber plummeted from the clouds, trailing fire and smoke.

We had actually shot down a British airplane.

TIME TO KILL

I FELT SICK. I SLUMPED AGAINST THE RADAR MACHINE that searched the skies for targets. *We had shot down a British airplane.* *I* had shot down a British airplane! Maybe not all by myself, but I had helped. Was the artillery shell that hit the bomber one of the ones I had hauled over? Simon had been shot down just like this, by an antiaircraft emplacement outside Berlin, and now I had done the same thing to someone else. I didn't know how many RAF officers were on that bomber. Were they already dead, or were they parachuting into enemy territory? Whichever it was, I'd killed them, whether it was now or later.

I'd joked with Simon that I had a deal with Allied bombers. I didn't shoot at them, and they didn't shoot at me. But now I *had* shot at them. It had always been a kind of joke, but deep down I'd really believed it—that no British bomb would ever kill me.

Now all deals were off.

Another bomb hit the same building across the street, cratering the lot and knocking us all off our feet. I hauled myself up on the radar machine, and found myself staring at a panel of knobs and readouts for calibrating the thing. I did the German Look to make sure I was alone, then twisted every dial I could way out of position. If we hit anything now, it would be by complete and utter accident.

The AA gun kept up a steady pace. *Poom. Poom. Poom. Poom.* At optimum speed, we were supposed to be getting off fifteen to twenty rounds per minute, but because it was our first night—and because we were all thirteen to seventeen years old—it was probably more like five to seven rounds per minute. But that was still too many shots at British bombers for my taste.

I snuck another peek at my watch. 3:27. I still had time to kill—which I suddenly realized was a very bad way of putting it.

"You're missing everything!" one of the boys told Fritz, and I smiled to myself. My sabotage had worked! I would have to be sure to always do that before the planes came.

One of the older SRD boys—I think his name was Ottmar—laughed. "Come on, Quex! How do you expect to kill that scientist if you can't even shoot down a plane?"

One of Ottmar's buddies—Erhard, I think, though I was always getting the two boys confused—laughed and punched Ottmar in the shoulder.

I fumbled the handoff of my next artillery shell. Kill a scientist? What were they talking about?

Fritz did the German Look. He caught me gaping at them and shot Ottmar (Erhard?) an angry frown, as if to say, *See? Be quiet! People are listening!* They went back to work, and I slipped around to the other side of the AA gun to think.

Was *that* what Fritz and Max and, I guessed, Erhard and Ottmar, had been pulled away to do? Was that what the "science team" meant? That they were training to ... what, assassinate some scientist somewhere?

And then a deeper thought struck me with all the force of an Allied bomb.

Fritz and Max and Ottmar and Erhard were the assassins my parents were looking for, and an Allied scientist was their target.

I was lost in thought when Max appeared in front of me. "I know why we're not hitting anything," he snarled. "Because *you* sabotaged the radar machine!"

HEAD CINEMA

I PUT MY HANDS UP. "NO, WAIT," I TOLD MAX. "I DIDN'T DO anything."

Max took a step toward me, and I took two steps back. "I saw you," he said. "You twisted the knobs. You did it on purpose!"

I did the German Look, hoping nobody else had heard him. Max and I were on the other side of the AA gun, the thundering, booming AA gun, and nobody else was around. But any minute, Max was going to tell the others.

Unless I went on the offensive.

I lunged for Max, grabbing his right arm and twisting it behind his back. He cried out in pain, then started to holler for help. I wrenched his arm up higher.

"Don't," I said, "or I'll break it."

Max writhed in my grip. "You'll never get away with this!" he said. He was probably right, but I didn't see any other way out.

"Who's the scientist you're supposed to kill?" I asked.

Max went still, and I felt light-headed. So I'd been right. Fritz and Max and Ottmar and Erhard *had* been training to kill an Allied scientist!

"I don't know what you're talking about," Max said.

I twisted his arm. "Tell me."

Max cried out. I glanced around, but we were still alone, the big AA gun shielding us from being heard or seen. For now.

"Okay. Okay! It's some Jewish scientist," Max spat out.

"*Who?*" I said, wrenching his arm again.

"Goldsmit! Hendrik Goldsmit."

"When? Where?"

"At some science conference somewhere! I don't know. They haven't told us where or when. I swear!"

"Why you? Why Fritz? Or Erhard? Or Ottmar?"

"I—I don't know," Max said. "Maybe because I can speak English."

I was surprised. "You speak English?"

Max swore at me in the King's English, and I had to admit he was pretty good at it.

My mind reeled. I had to tell my parents a man named Hendrik Goldsmit was the target as soon as I could. But I had to meet Simon first, help him get out of Berlin. What time was it? And what was I going to do about Max?

Max took advantage of my reverie. He slammed the heel of his boot down on my toe, making me jump back. He twisted himself around and slipped free, clutching at his injured arm as he staggered back from me.

I could run now, get away while the others had to stay at their post, but then Max would rat me out and my whole career as a spy would be over. I could never come back. I'd have to leave Germany with Simon, if that was even possible. And what about my parents? How would they get out of Berlin? Would they be captured? Killed?

Worse?

The Germans have a great word for seeing everything that can go wrong play out in your head. They call it *Kopfkino* — "head cinema." And what I saw playing out on the movie screen in my head was the end of everything.

I yanked my Hitler Youth dagger from its sheath.

Max's eyes went wide, as if he couldn't believe I might really be an enemy agent, even though he'd caught me sabotaging the gun. He fumbled at the snap on his dagger's sheath. I should have jumped him then, but I hesitated. Could I really do this? Could I really kill another person in cold blood?

Max drew his dagger. Took a step toward me.

And then Max exploded.

A huge piece of shrapnel, the shredded tip of a destroyed British bomber's wing, we later found out, fell out of the sky and ripped Max in two like he was made of paper.

But Max wasn't made of paper. He was made of flesh and blood and bone that exploded all over me and knocked me to the ground.

One second he was there, snarling at me, and the next second he was just . . . gone.

The horror of what I'd seen — what I would never, *ever* be able to *un*see — made me vomit and collapse to my knees. The stink of blood and guts and vomit filled my head, and I thought I was going to pass out. I was shaking so badly I almost couldn't move, but I had to get as far away from the carnage as I could. I dragged myself around to the other side of the gun, where the other boys were still working.

Fritz saw me covered with blood and ran to me. I pointed to the other side of the AA gun, and some of the boys went to look. They came back crying and pale, and more than one of them bent over the AA gun's spidery legs to wretch.

I shook with both horror and guilt. I had wanted to keep Max from telling on me for sabotaging the AA gun, for pumping him for information about the science team, and now he was dead. It was hard not to think I'd caused it somehow, that my wishing him quiet had killed him.

Dully, I remembered that I was supposed to be somewhere else. I wiped Max's blood from the glass on my wristwatch. 3:40! It would take me longer than five minutes to get to my rendezvous with Simon. I was going to be late.

I turned to go.

And that was when the Edelweiss Pirates attacked.

PIRATES OF THE EDELWEISS

THE EDELWEISS PIRATES CAME STREAMING OUT OF A
nearby alley, screaming, "Eternal war with the Hitler Youth!"

The AA gun team was still reeling from Max's death, and we
were slow to understand what was going on. The Edelweiss Pirates
were on us before we could think, attacking with clubs and
broken bottles and daggers. The SRD had been conducting
more and more raids on the cinemas and pool halls and pubs
where the Edelweiss Pirates hung out all day, and this was their
payback — attacking us when we least expected it, when the numbers were in their favor.

"Sorry if it hurts, mates, sorry we can't stay," they sang,
"We're Edelweiss Pirates, and we're on our way.
We march by banks of Ruhr and Rhine
And smash the Hitler Youth in twain,
Our song is freedom, love, and life,
We're Pirates of the Edelweiss!"

A boy hit me in the back with a table leg, and I crumpled to the ground. It was the wake-up call I needed. My shock over Max's death washed away like blood under peroxide, replaced by the adrenaline rush of a fistfight. The Pirate came at me again and I swept out a leg, knocking him to the ground. I threw myself on top of him before he could get up again, pinning the hand that held the table leg to the ground. He looked up at me in abject horror, probably because I was covered in Max's blood and guts. I used his momentary shock to crack a fist across his face, and he passed out. As I climbed up off him, I was surprised to realize I recognized him—he was the boy who'd run off crying when he was kicked out of the Hitler Youth trials because of his asthma.

All around me, the AA gun team was swarmed by Edelweiss Pirates. Like me, the rest of the Hitler Youth boys had started slow and wobbly, but just as quickly their weakness had been knocked out of them. They were fighting back in earnest now, many of them with their Hitler Youth daggers in hand. I snatched mine up from where I'd dropped it and checked my watch. 3:46! I was officially late, and I hadn't even left yet. Simon would be standing in the shadows of the alley, hoping not to be caught by a passing air raid patrol while he waited for me. I had to get to him!

I threaded my way through the melee, stopping to defend myself against a boy with a broken bottle. I had just driven him off when I saw Fritz surrounded by three Edelweiss Pirates. Two of them had clubs, and the other had a knife. Fritz was doing everything I'd taught him to do in a fight — right stance, right balance, right defensive position — but not even I could fend off three boys like that, especially if they were all a head taller than me, as they were to little three-cheeses-tall Fritz. If somebody didn't help him, he was going to get really hurt. Maybe even killed.

I glanced at my watch again, and back at Fritz. Fritz, who hadn't talked to me in days. Fritz, who threw himself into pool halls looking for fights. *Fritz, who was part of a secret mission to kill a Jewish scientist.*

Fritz, who had saved my life.

I cursed in German, then in English, and threw myself at the boy with the knife. I drove him headfirst into the paved street, and he howled. Fritz had already gone after one of the other two, ducking a swing from the boy's club and jabbing at his leg with his dagger. I ran at the remaining boy from the side, knocking him to the ground. He swung his club at me and it glanced off the side of my head. My temple exploded with pain. I put a hand to the throbbing, tender lump on my head and rolled away. The Pirate twisted and raised his club to hit me again, but he screamed and jolted as if someone had just stuck a cattle prod in his back. It was Fritz. He kicked the boy in the back again, and the Pirate dropped his club and writhed in pain.

Fritz reached down and helped me up. He didn't look as wild or bloodthirsty as he had when he'd led the pool hall raid or the attack on Herr Professor Doktor Major Melcher. He looked cold. Hard. The exploding bombs, the AA gun, the evisceration of Max, the ambush by the Edelweiss Pirates—this was *war*. We weren't playing games anymore, and we both knew it.

"Thanks," I told him.

"You too," he said.

Fritz ran to help another Hitler Youth beset by Edelweiss Pirates, and I looked at my watch. 4:02. I was very, very late now.

I ran.

GONE

IT TOOK ME ONLY TEN MINUTES TO RUN WHAT WOULD usually have taken me fifteen, even dodging all the fires and craters and piles of rubble in the streets. But it didn't matter.

When I got to the rendezvous point, Simon was already gone.

OPERATION PAPERCLIP

I SAT WITH MY MOTHER AND FATHER IN DA'S OFFICE, waiting for word that Simon had somehow reached the next rendezvous point outside Berlin. He hadn't come back to the embassy last night, which meant he'd tried to make it on his own.

Or he'd been captured.

The morning sun was just breaking through the smog of dust and smoke that hung over the city. I hadn't slept since I'd come home from the air raid. I'd been too worried about Simon. Too guilt-stricken over missing my appointment.

Da and Ma had understood, had told me it wasn't my fault. That they had expected too much of me. But that only made it worse. I *wanted* to be able to handle whatever they asked me to do, and more. I wanted to be better than everybody thought I was. I wanted them to think of me as an adult, not a kid who couldn't cut it.

"Hendrik Goldsmit. Hendrik Goldsmit," Ma said, pacing the floor. She was as worried as I was that Simon had been captured, but she had turned her nervous energy to the problem of the lead I'd brought home. The one thing I'd done right all night. "Goldsmit's a physicist. Dutch. Got out of the Netherlands right before Hitler invaded. He works for the Americans now, on their atomic bomb project."

"What's an atomic bomb?" I asked.

Ma shook her head. "Some kind of . . . superbomb. I've only heard rumors. It may not even be possible. But if it is, it'll change everything. Even more than that jet fighter."

I shrank farther into my chair at the mention of the jet fighter plans, which might be in the hands of the Nazis right now. Along with Simon.

"The real question," said Ma, "is how in the world the Nazis think they can assassinate Goldsmit when he's in some secret military laboratory in the States."

"Here! I knew I'd read his name recently," Da said. He'd been combing through old issues of the Nazi newspapers he'd saved and had finally found the article he'd been looking for. "There's a science conference in the Swiss Alps in two days' time, and Goldsmit's supposed to be there."

Ma grabbed up the newspaper and read the article.

"But . . . why would an Allied scientist come to Switzerland in the middle of the war?" I asked.

"Exchange of ideas, progress of science," Da suggested.

"Operation Paperclip," Ma said under her breath.

"Operation what?" I said.

"Paperclip. A secret Allied operation to recruit—or kidnap, if necessary—Nazi scientists. He must be coming here to recruit someone at the conference!"

"He should be perfectly safe," Da said. "The Germans would never strike inside Switzerland's borders. It would violate their neutrality."

Ma snorted. "The Nazis don't care a fig for neutrality. Just ask Denmark. The only reason the Nazis don't attack Switzerland is because tanks don't go up mountains."

Switzerland had declared its neutrality right at the start of the war, just like Spain and Sweden. And Ireland. But tiny Switzerland was right on Germany's southern border, wedged in between Occupied France and Fascist Italy. Germany had left Switzerland alone for now, going around the Alps instead of through them. They probably figured Switzerland would just give in when Germany took over the rest of the world.

"In any event," Ma said, "the Swiss aren't about to let any German soldiers in."

"Which is why the Nazis are sending *children*," Da said with disgust.

"The science team," I said.

"It's brilliant," Ma said. "The Swiss will let them right in, and then they can assassinate Goldsmit."

"We have to get word to British Intelligence," I said.

"The conference is in two days," Ma said. "We can't possibly get a message out in time. By the time London gets our diplomatic packet, Goldsmit will already be at the conference—and it will take even longer to get word to him or anybody else who can help."

"Best I could do is call up London and just tell them," Da said. "But you know as well as I do that the phones are bugged. The Gestapo would be on us before we could make it out the front door."

"But—we can't just let them kill him!" I said. After being the one to discover who the Nazis were planning to assassinate, I didn't want what I'd learned from Max to mean nothing after all.

The phone rang, and I jumped.

It had to be someone calling about Simon.

THE MISSING WINE

DA SNATCHED THE PHONE RECEIVER UP AND LISTENED.

"Yes, she's right here," he said, and handed the phone to my mother.

"Yes?" she said in German. "I see. I see. Yes, it's all right. You can deliver the wine another time, then. Yes. Thanks." She set the receiver down and took a deep breath. "Simon didn't make the riverboat that was to take him to Oranienburg," Ma said, decoding her conversation for us. "He must have been captured."

Simon's ship had literally sailed without him. My stomach folded in on itself, and tears sprang to my eyes. I couldn't help it. It wasn't just because I liked Simon, thought of him like a brother. It was because it was *my fault* he'd been captured. If the shrapnel hadn't hit Max. If the Edelweiss Pirates hadn't attacked. If I hadn't stopped to help Fritz. I replayed the whole night in my head, trying to make it come out differently each time. But every time it was the same. Every time I ended up in that alleyway alone, hands on my knees, tears in my eyes, blood on my hands.

Ma put a hand on my shoulder. I was about to fall into her arms, cry into her shoulder the way I had when I was a little boy and fell and scraped my knee. But before she could put her arms around me, the air raid sirens howled again. It was the Americans' turn to bomb us.

I stood wearily from my chair and dragged a bloodstained sleeve across my eyes. I had an AA gun to man.

"No, Michael!" Da said. "You can't go out again! Not after last night. You need rest. A bath. Bed."

"I have to," I told him. "They'll notice if I'm gone. They'll report me."

"Then let them report you! We should never have brought him here with us," Da told Ma. "He's too young. The war's been too hard on him. We should have left him in Ireland."

"No!" I said. "No! I can do this! I just—I just messed up last night. I'm sorry. I have to go."

I staggered out the back door, mostly so I wouldn't have to leave with my parents and the staff through the front door and let them see me cry.

I wanted to be here, in Berlin, working as a spy. Helping the Allies. If I'd stayed back home in Ireland, I would just be in school, maybe helping collect rubber and paper and metal for the war effort. I wouldn't be helping the Allies bomb factories or steal secret jet fighter plans.

But now they weren't going to get the plans. The blueprints for Projekt 1065 had been lost with Simon. Unless I could reconstruct them. Redraw them from memory. Words and numbers and images flashed by in my head. Could I do it? Could I remember all of it? I didn't know if I could without Simon.

A dark figure lunged at me from the shadows in the alley behind the embassy. I started to cry out, but the man slapped a hand over my mouth. I looked up at him, and my eyes went wide.

It was Simon!

EINBAHNSTRASSE

SIMON LOOKED SHRUNKEN AND PALE. HE BENT OVER double at the waist, a hand wrapped around his stomach like he'd eaten a bad bratwurst. I immediately turned him toward the back door and helped him climb the stairs. The staff had already cleared out because of the air raid. That's why Simon had waited until then to come back to the house. I led him to the little hidden closet at the back of Da's office, signaled for him to wait (as if he could go anywhere), and ran to catch my parents before they went down into the bunker. I was so giddy I was practically hopping. I couldn't believe it—Simon was alive! I hadn't gotten him captured by the Gestapo after all.

"Da! Ma!" I cried. The staff was with them, and everybody stopped to find out what was wrong. I panted from my run, trying to think how to tell them Simon was back without alerting the staff.

"That—that wine you were trying to have delivered," I said, remembering the coded conversation Ma had had with her contact on the phone. "It made it after all. They left it at the back door."

Da and Ma shared a startled look.

"I'll see to it," said Mrs. Keller, the housekeeper.

"No, no!" Da said. "No, I forbid any of the staff to risk their lives over a case of wine, no matter how expensive it is. Get to the bunkers. Michael and I'll see to it."

Mrs. Keller and the others protested, but Da sent them away. Ma gave us a hopeful look before going with the staff to make sure none of them came back. Da and I rushed back to the secret closet, where Simon lay slumped against the bookcases.

"Good God, are we happy to see you," Da said. "What happened?"

Simon told us how he'd waited at the rendezvous point for me past our meeting time, and my ears burned hot with shame. I started to apologize, but Simon held up a hand.

"I heard a patrol coming, so I decided to try to make it on my own. I'd studied the maps. I thought I could do it. I made it halfway across the city, but at some point I must have made a wrong turn. I was supposed to be on Friedrichstrasse, but instead, I somehow ended up on Einbahnstrasse. I doubled back, trying to find Friedrichstrasse, and that's when they spotted me."

Da and I glanced at each other, and I wondered which of us was going to be the first to tell him.

"What?" Simon asked.

"That probably *was* Friedrichstrasse," Da told him.

"No! I'm telling you, the sign said, *Einbahnstrasse*."

"*Einbahnstrasse* means 'one-way street,'" I explained. "That *was* Friedrichstrasse. You just saw the sign that said it was one way, not the sign with the street name on it."

Simon closed his eyes and thunked his head back against the bookshelves. "Well. I suppose I should have learned a little more German while I was holed up here, shouldn't I?"

Simon told us a Hitler Youth patrol had spotted him, and when he didn't heed their calls they chased him through the streets.

"Almost lost them," he said. "But one of the boys stayed on my tail. Cornered me in an alley. He couldn't have been more than ten years old. I had my pistol, but I'm afraid I didn't have it in me to shoot him. He was just a boy. He didn't have any similar reservations about using his dagger on me, though."

Simon pulled his hand away from his stomach. His shirt and hand were covered with blood.

"Good God! Why didn't you say something?" Da said, and he went for the alcohol and bandages.

"What about the plans?" I asked Simon.

He pulled them out from inside his shirt. "A little bloody, but still intact, I think," he said.

I sighed with relief. Simon was alive, and the plans were safe. His ship may have sailed, but Ma could arrange another one in time.

Da came back with the medical kit. Bombs began to fall outside, shaking the books on the shelves.

"Ah," Simon said as Da bandaged him. "They're playing my song."

"I have to get to the bunker, or someone from the staff will come looking for me," Da said.

"I'll be fine with Michael," Simon replied. "I can talk him through patching me up."

"We're glad you're still alive," Da said, shaking Simon's hand.

"So am I, as it happens," said Simon.

Da left, and Simon peeled back his torn and bloody shirt. I paled.

"Simon, I'm so sorry," I told him. Tears sprang to my eyes. "I should have been there. I shouldn't have — "

Simon put up a hand. "I've never once been part of a covert action that went according to plan," he said. He waved his hand to encompass himself and the little closet he was hidden in. "Case in point: how I got here in the first place. I'm sure you would have been there if you could."

Simon showed me how to clean his wound, which he bore with gritted teeth.

"We figured out who's going to be assassinated," I said to distract him. I told him all about Goldsmit and the science conference, Fritz and the so-called science team.

"It's your little friend who's going to be doing the assassinating?" Simon said.

I nodded. "And there's no time to get word back to London. The conference is in two days."

"Which means you've got to get on that science team," Simon said. "You have to go to Switzerland and stop it yourself."

AN OPENING
ON THE TEAM

I FROZE. "WHAT? ME, JOIN THE SCIENCE TEAM? BUT—BUT
how?"

"You said this boy, Max, he was a part of the team, but he was
killed."

I felt the blood drain out of my head and my skin crawl as I saw
it again, the shrapnel falling, slicing into Max, the blood, the guts . . .

"Yes," I said quietly. "He was killed."

"So there's an opening on the team," Simon said.

Yes. Yes! Simon was right! With Max dead, they would be
looking to replace him on the team.

"That's true," I told Simon, breathless. "And Max said he was
on the team because he could speak English!"

"Which you do *almost* as well as an Englishman," Simon said,
poking a little fun to disguise his discomfort.

I nodded. I could do this. I could join the science team with
Fritz. And I didn't know how yet, but I could stop whatever it

was they were planning. I had to. No matter what Simon said, it was my fault he hadn't made it out of Berlin. My fault he'd been stabbed by a Hitler Youth boy on patrol. My fault he was cooped up again in the secret closet in my father's study.

I was going to prove that he and my parents could trust me the next time they needed me.

I just had to get onto that team.

I heard the *pok-pok-pok* of the antiaircraft guns. My troop would already be at their stations.

"They may already be choosing a replacement!" I said. "I have to get to my AA gun."

"Go," Simon told me. "Go—I'll be fine. Just do whatever it takes to get yourself on that team!"

THE MAN FROM NANTUCKET

I SPENT THE ENTIRE AIR RAID RECITING ENGLISH limericks.

"There once was a farmer from Leeds, who swallowed a packet of seeds," I sang as I hauled ammunition to the AA gun. "It soon came to pass he was covered with grass, but has all the tomatoes he needs!"

The other boys stared at me as though I was insane. My jokes were bombing more than the airplanes overhead. I had to admit, they might have gone over better if any of them understood English. I carried on undaunted.

"There once was a man from Nantucket, who kept all his cash in a bucket. But his daughter named Nan ran away with a man, and as for the bucket, Nantucket!"

I laughed at my own joke, which got me more stares.

"Wait. Here's another," I said, handing off another round for the 88. "A funny old bird is the pelican. His beak can hold more than his belly can. He can take in his beak enough food for a week, but I don't know how the helican!"

Fritz pulled me aside. "What are you doing?" he asked me in German.

What I was doing was trying to remind SS-Obersturmführer Trumbauer that I was fluent in English, in case he had forgotten. The SS man was there, overseeing our AA gun. But I couldn't explain that to Fritz. I just went back to work.

Dozens more limericks and Englishman, Scotsman, and Irishman jokes later, the air raid was over. We had survived round two with the Allied bombers.

I had just started to sing "Danny Boy" for everybody when SS-Obersturmführer Trumbauer had us line up for our orders.

"Sir, yes, sir!" I said in English, and I gave my most enthusiastic salute. "Heil Hitler!"

Trumbauer nodded at me. Fritz looked at me strangely.

"It's time to march," Trumbauer said. "We will only go to the bridge and back, so we are not too far away should there be another air raid."

"Sir?" Fritz said. "Am I excused to work on our special SRD training?"

Special *assassination* training, he meant. I knew that now.

"Yes, of course, Quex," SS-Obersturmführer Trumbauer said. "And we need to select a replacement for Max after he died for Germany, don't we?"

I licked my lips. *Here we go*, I thought. My chance to join the science team.

"Train well, Fritz!" I said in English. I pretended to catch myself, and smacked my forehead. "I'm sorry!" I said in German. "Sometimes I forget and just say things in English. It is my first language, after all."

Fritz gave me another confused look. I admit, I was being pretty obvious about it. But I didn't want Trumbauer to pass me over.

Trumbauer walked down the line toward me. I stood tall. Stuck out my chest.

And the SS man walked right past me.

"Horst Fortner, step forward," SS-Obersturmführer Trumbauer said. "You have been selected for an elite SRD mission."

Horst? *Horst?* The donkey-faced ogre from our Jungvolk group? How in the world could he be selected for the science team over me? He didn't know a word of English, and he was proud of it!

Horst jumped out of the line and threw his arm into the air in a fervent Nazi salute. "Thank you, SS-Obersturmführer Trumbauer! I would die for the Fatherland!"

"I know you would, Horst," Trumbauer said with an appreciative nod. "Please join Fritz. He will show you to the training ground."

"Heil Hitler!" Horst yelled, and Trumbauer returned the salute.

"Are—are you sure you don't want me instead?" I blurted out in German. Fritz turned with a frown, as if I was being a fool to speak out when I wasn't supposed to. I probably was. But I needed to join that team.

"I am quite confident in the choice I have made, Mr. O'Shaunessey," SS-Obersturmführer Trumbauer said icily. Fritz gave me a quick shake of the head and turned back to Trumbauer, waiting to be dismissed. I cursed inwardly. How was I going to get on that science team?

"Just be sure that the two of you are back this afternoon," SS-Obersturmführer Trumbauer told them. "We have been invited to a very special event." Whatever it was, it was so special he swelled with joy. Trumbauer was practically glowing. I wondered if the Nazis had finally gotten so desperate they were going to give us tanks and turn us loose on the Allies.

But no, it was worse. Much, much worse.

"This afternoon — " SS-Obersturmführer Trumbauer told us, "this afternoon, we have the great and glorious honor of hearing the Führer speak to us *in person!*"

EVIL LEPRECHAUN

WE STOOD IN A STREET OUTSIDE THE OLD REICH Chancellery. Adolf Hitler ruled the German nation from this building, just as the president of the Weimar Republic had before him, and the emperor of Prussia before him. The main building was all white columns and tall windows and black gabled roof. Like the country house of a European king. Connected to it were modern buildings added by the Nazis: square, gray towers with flat roofs, which housed the administrative clerks and officials that formed the octopus-like arms of the government. The Nazis loved their *Amtsschimmel*. Their "bureaucratic mildew." The stacks and stacks of government paperwork they used to document every little thing. In English we called it "red tape." If the Allies managed to hit the Reich Chancellery with a bomb, it wouldn't rain brick and ash. It would rain burning papers.

But the chancellery still looked immaculate. I didn't know how they did it. It was brilliant white in a city filled with dust and gray smoke, and covered in crisp, clean, red, white, and black swastika flags. But the more I stared at the building, the more I realized there was something off. Most of the flags hung from the usual places—beneath awnings and under windows and over arched walkways. But some of the flags hung in odd places, like between windows and on the roof. One of the oddly placed flags fluttered in the wind, and I saw behind it the wall was cracked and crumbling. The Reich Chancellery *had* taken damage from Allied bombs after all. The Nazis had just draped swastikas over the damage, hiding it the same way they covered up their recent defeats in Stalingrad and Northern Africa.

SS officers surrounded us. Members of Hitler's personal guard. The boys around me grew tense. Straighter. Stood taller. Even I caught myself straining to see around the guards. To see Hitler in person, the great boogyman that had bedeviled Europe and the rest of the world, was like catching a glimpse of a leprechaun. A very, very evil leprechaun.

But it wasn't Hitler who pushed through the guards—it was Artur Axmann, the head of the Hitler Youth. You could almost feel a silent, collective groan from the boys. None of us had met Axmann, but none of us particularly wanted to. He was the one who wrote all the ridiculous speeches and silly directives that our youth leaders read to us during our weekly Hitler Youth meetings.

Axmann looked as dumb as his weekly pronouncements, like a thug in an officer's uniform.

"Welcome. Welcome," Axmann said quickly. "This is a great day for you. A great day indeed. To meet me, and meet the Führer. I hope you all appreciate what an honor this is. You will tell your grandchildren of this day. I may be your inspiration, your mentor, your second father, but the superimposing leader of all desires of youth is Adolf Hitler."

I fought a powerful urge to roll my eyes.

And then the Führer himself was there. Adolf Hitler.

HITLER

ADOLF HITLER WAS A FEW INCHES SHORTER THAN ALL OF his guards. The first thing you noticed about him was his pale face and his long, ratlike nose with that bushy little mustache under it. His dark brown hair swept down across his forehead to just above his eyes, which were baggy and tired-looking. Maybe it was from the long hours spent running a world war. Or maybe he couldn't sleep for all the bombs the Allies dropped on him day and night. He wore the brown uniform and red swastika armband of the German army, but unlike everybody else in Germany who were so mad for medals that they bought them from shops, Hitler wore only one: the Iron Cross First Class he'd won for bravery in World War I. (I knew because I'd had to memorize that fact to pass my Hitler Youth initiation.)

Hitler blinked in the bright sunlight of the late winter afternoon like a hedgehog emerging from hibernation.

"Heil Hitler!" Axmann cried.

We all overcame our momentary astonishment at seeing the Führer in person and threw our right arms in the air. "Heil Hitler!" we cried. I felt like a traitor, but this was no time to take a stand. I had to pretend to love him the same way everybody else did.

Hitler smiled at us like an affectionate old grandfather.

"Your name, my Führer, is the happiness of youth," Axmann said. "Your name, my Führer, is for us everlasting life!"

He was laying it on a bit thick, I thought, but Hitler must have been used to it from everybody he met. He nodded to Axmann, which somehow also seemed to communicate that it was time for him to shut up. Axmann took the hint and faded back among the towering elite SS guards.

Hitler looked out over us. Now each and every one of us really was standing as straight and tall as we could get. Even me. I needed to blend in, it was true, but there was something about the man that made you want to appear perfect in his eyes.

Maybe it was fear.

"We older ones are used up," Hitler said. He spoke so softly at first that we had to lean in to hear him—which was a good trick, I realized. "We are rotten to the marrow. We are cowardly and sentimental."

"No!" some of the boys called out. Hitler held up a hand to quiet them.

"It is true. We adults bear the burden of a humiliating past, and have in our blood the dull recollection of serfdom and servility. But my magnificent youngsters!" Hitler said, gazing out lovingly at all of us. "Are there any finer ones in the world? Look at these young men and boys. What material! With you, I can make a new world. This is the heroic stage of youth. Out of it will come the creative man, the man-god. *You.*"

A tingle thrilled through me, despite how much I hated him. To hear someone tell you that you will rebuild the world, that you will be a hero, a *man-god*, was a powerful thing. I wanted to do all that. To *be* all that. Just not for Hitler and the Nazis.

"You, my youth, are our nation's most precious guarantee for a great future." Hitler's voice rose as he went on. "The Thousand-Year Reich. You are destined to be the leaders of a glorious new order under the supremacy of National Socialism. Never forget that one day, you will rule the world!"

The boys around me broke out in a spontaneous "*Sieg Heil!*"

"Learn, while you are still young, that life for you must mean sacrifice: sacrifice of your personal freedom, sacrifice of your free time, sacrifice of many of the small pleasures of life."

I turned to look at Fritz, who stood beside me. He wasn't looking at Hitler just then. He had his eyes to the ground just beyond the Führer, as though something Hitler said had him lost in thought.

"To do so, you must be violently active. Dominating. Intrepid. *Brutal.*" Hitler's voice rose and fell, ebbing and flowing like the Irish Sea. It was captivating. Impossible to ignore. "Youth must be indifferent to pain. There must be no weakness in you. No tenderness. You must learn to do without, to endure criticism and injustice, to be reliable, discreet, decent, and loyal. You must be as swift as greyhounds. Tough as leather. As hard as Krupp steel!"

I noticed Hitler didn't say anything about being smart. Intelligence had no place in the Hitler Youth. Or in Nazi Germany, for that matter. But Fritz was nodding emphatically beside me. Whatever it was he'd been thinking about, he'd made up his mind.

Hitler started in on how the tide of the war would soon turn in Germany's favor again, and I tuned out. From the corner of my eye, I watched Fritz and Horst and Ottmar and Erhard, the four boys on the science team. They quivered as Hitler spoke, like five-year-olds so anxious to open their presents on Christmas morning they were going to puke. They were euphoric. Ecstatic. They could barely control themselves. Tears filled their eyes. Not everyone was like that, I realized. Everyone was a little awestruck, but those four looked like they were about to drop to their knees and kiss the ground Hitler walked on. Every time he talked about tossing Germany's enemies back into the sea or smashing the Russians, they were the first and the loudest to shout "Heil Hitler!"

And that's when I finally understood. That's when I knew why Fritz and Horst and Ottmar and Erhard were on the science team.

And why I wasn't.

SUPER-NAZIS

"THEY'RE FANATICS!" I TOLD SIMON. AFTER GETTING HOME from the Hitler rally, I'd burst into my house and run straight to the secret room. "That's why they were recruited. Because they're *zealots*. You should have seen these four guys. It was like God himself had come down from on high to talk to them. I saw it in their faces. Heard it in their shouts. It's like a religion for them. They *believe* Hitler's nonsense. Aryan supremacy. The Jewish threat. World domination. All of it."

"So speaking English has nothing to do with it," Simon said.

"No. They love Hitler so much they would do anything for him. Kill for him. *Die* for him. To get on that team, all I have to do is prove to them I'm a super-Nazi. I just don't know how."

Simon nodded. "I know how," he said. "You have to turn me in."

NO JOKE

YOU HAVE TO TURN ME IN.

Simon's words hung in the air like a bomb, waiting to explode.

"No," I said. "Never!"

My parents joined us in the secret room, and Simon told them his idea.

"I won't do it!" I said. "I can't! It would ruin everything! What about Projekt 1065? If Simon's caught, the Allies will never get the jet fighter plans."

"You'll have to take those with you to Switzerland," Simon said. "You can give them to Professor Goldsmit to take back to the Allies after you stop his assassination."

I threw my hands up. Because that wouldn't be dangerous at all. If I got caught with the plans for Projekt 1065, I wouldn't even make it to Switzerland to save Goldsmit. But that wasn't nearly the biggest problem with this plan.

"You'll get in trouble too," I told my parents. "They'll know you hid him here."

Da nodded. Ma sat down slowly in Da's desk chair. They were on the fence, I could tell. But the fact that they were even considering this was crazy.

I stood and went to my parents. "We can't do this!" I said to Ma. "You told me before, it's too valuable to give up everything you've worked for just for one man, and Goldsmit's just one man."

"One man who may know how to build an atomic bomb," Ma said. "Not to mention that this could finally get those jet fighter plans into the hands of the Allies. We just have to decide if it's worth trading one for the other."

"The decision is whether or not we can put our son in that kind of danger," Da said.

"He can do it. I know he can," Simon said.

It's what I'd wanted to hear — what I'd longed to hear. That I was good enough to be a proper spy. But now I didn't want it. Not if it meant giving up Simon to the Nazis.

"Michael, you have to save Professor Goldsmit," Simon said. "The only way you can do it is to get on that team, and the only way you can get on that team is to do something so radical they automatically promote you, like the boy who turned in his parents. And you'll be doing him one better — you'll be turning in a British spy who also just happens to be a Jew."

I shook my head. I felt sick, like I might throw up. Or cry. I'd had fun sneaking around and writing coded messages. Memorizing the plans for Projekt 1065 had been fun too. Up until now, it had all been a game. Kim's Game. The game of spies. But if I turned

Simon in, if I turned my *parents* in, this wouldn't be a game any-more. This would be real. We were talking about real sacrifice here—and not my sacrifice. The sacrifice of people I loved and cared about.

"You'll be sent to a concentration camp," I told my parents, my voice cracking.

"No," Da said. "We'll be long gone."

I frowned. What was he talking about?

"I want out, Michael," Da said. "I want all of us out. It's too dangerous. The tide has turned with the German defeat at Stalingrad. The Nazis are like cornered animals. Savage. Wild. Putting thirteen-year-olds in charge of antiaircraft guns, sending seventeen-year-olds to the front lines. I don't know how much longer the war will last—another year? Two? Three? But the longer it lasts, the more abominable the Nazis will become. One way or another, we will die if we stay here. I've already talked it over with your mother."

Ma nodded, her lips pursed. "We were going to put in for a transfer," she explained. "But if we turn Simon in to get Michael on the team, there won't be time for that. We'll have to sneak out. I'll get in touch with my network. By the time Simon is taken into 'protective custody,' your father and I will have disappeared. It'll make us look more the guilty, anyhow, and you more the hero."

"But you said it would take weeks to set up another escape route for Simon," I said, desperately trying to find a logical rea-son to cancel this crazy plan. "And now *you're* going to escape?"

"Yes," Ma said. "We'll be winging it, to be sure. But I know the network, and the both of us know the territory." Da nodded at her. "Simon didn't. And we have diplomatic immunity, which might count for something if we're caught."

"It's the Nazis! Diplomatic immunity won't count for anything, and you know it! If you're caught, you'll be killed!" I was on the verge of tears again.

"We'll be killed if we stay," Da said.

I paced restlessly. "And Simon?" I asked.

Simon bowed his head. No one else answered the question, so I did for them.

"*He'll* be sent to a concentration camp," I said.

I saw it all in my "head cinema." Torture. Interrogation. Imprisonment. All the horrible things everybody knew happened at the concentration camps, but we didn't let ourselves think about.

Da signaled for me to sit and be quiet, and Ma went to the door to make sure none of the staff were listening in. I sat back down in my chair, my chest heaving. My hands balled into fists. I desperately wanted to hit something.

"Did you hear the one about the Englishman, the Irishman, and the Scotsman who were all sentenced to a year in prison?" Simon asked.

"I don't want to hear any jokes!" I told him. He was trying to calm me down, but I didn't want to be calm. "I'm not turning you in, Simon. It's not worth it."

Simon got serious. "Michael, the atomic bomb program is perhaps the most important project of the entire war. Maybe of all time. If this thing does what people think it will, it will change the way wars are fought. It will change the whole world. Far more than any jet fighter plans. Every night, the British drop tens of thousands of bombs on Berlin, and it still stands. With an atomic bomb, you drop just one, and it destroys an entire city. If there can be such a thing as an atomic bomb, it's vital the Allies build one first. And Professor Goldsmit is vital to its creation."

Da took a deep breath and nodded. "Then we do it."

Ma took my hand and nodded her agreement.

I couldn't believe what I was hearing. I pulled my hand away and stood, but I didn't yell. "No. I can't. I won't. There has to be another way," I told them, and I left to go find it.

A WALKING A-BOMB

PEOPLE STEPPED OFF THE SIDEWALK TO AVOID ME AS I walked through the streets of Berlin. I liked to think it was the angry aura around me, the clenched fists that told them not to bump into me, or there'd be a fight. That I was a walking atomic bomb, ready to go off and level this stinking city any second. The truth was, of course, it was the uniform that made them scared. But I pretended they could feel the rage coming off of me in waves. Like I could warp the world with my fury. I wished I could.

Turn in Simon. Send my parents on the run! How could they really think that was the answer? How did they really think I could do that? I had to find another way to get on that team.

My feet took me to Fritz's house before I even understood my idea. It wasn't a particularly good idea, but it was all I could think of, all that made it through the white noise of outrage screaming in my head like an air raid siren. Fritz was the answer. He had to be. He and I were friends. Of a sort. We had been friends once, briefly. True, over the last couple of weeks we'd grown apart. And not just because he'd been spending most of his free time with the science team. It was more than that. Fritz was changing. Becoming something . . . different. Something I didn't like. But that boy who'd asked me to help him be stronger, that boy who'd helped *me* be stronger, the boy who'd dragged me upstairs to share his detective novels with me, *that* boy — that friend — had to still be in there somewhere. And that friend would see the light. That friend would help me save the scientist.

Fritz's sister, Lina, met me at the door.

"Hello, future wife," I said. "Is my future brother-in-law at home?"

Lina didn't say a word but opened the door wider for me to come inside. She pointed not upstairs, where Fritz's room was, but down the first-floor hallway, to the back of the house.

I went down the hall to the kitchen at the back of the house, but Fritz wasn't there. I sniffed. I thought I smelled smoke, but the oven wasn't on, and there was nothing on the stove. I caught a glimpse of a dark gray cloud curling into the sky through the window in the back door, and I stepped outside.

Fritz was in the backyard, throwing his collection of detective novels into a bucket full of flames.

BOY-MEN

I THREW MYSELF ACROSS THE YARD, GRABBING THE book in Fritz's hand.

"What are you doing?" I cried. "Stop!"

Half his collection was already burning in the bucket. Fritz yanked the book back from me and tried to hold it over his head where I couldn't reach it, but I was taller than he was. I snatched at the book, and we wrestled over it for a few desperate seconds until at last I had it.

I was about to ask him again what the bloody hell he thought he was doing, when he punched me in the nose.

It was fast and straight and his feet were planted just right and I'd never seen it coming—all the things I'd taught him to do. I staggered back, lost my footing, and fell on my butt. I put a hand to my nose and came away with blood.

Fritz stood over me, a look of fierce cruelty in his knitted eyebrows, and suddenly I understood. Why Fritz had wanted me to teach him how to fight. Why he'd been so desperate to join the SRD. All his life, Fritz had been the boy with the bloody nose sitting here on the ground, looking up at the bully who'd beaten him.

He'd joined the SRD so he could become the bully himself. Just like little Hitler.

"So this is what it's come to," I said. I didn't get up. I didn't want to fight Fritz. That's not why I was here. "You'd burn these books," I said. I hurled the book I'd taken back at him, and he batted it away. "You'd burn something you love just to be on top for once in your life. Even if it means turning your back on who you are."

Fritz tugged at his SRD uniform. "This *is* who I am. I'm going to lead Germany into the future. I'm going to help Hitler rule the world. But to do that, I have to make sacrifices," he said, quoting the Führer back to me. "You've burned books too. You made me burn books, that day the other boys attacked me!"

"I told you to burn those books so the other boys wouldn't *kill* you!"

"No," Fritz said. He picked up the book I'd thrown at him. "They were right. This is degenerate *filth*. I should never have read it to begin with. And neither should you. A good Nazi doesn't need books or philosophy or art. We think with our *blood*."

"You think with your *blood*?" I said. "What does that even mean? How is that even possible?"

Fritz threw the book back at me, but I ducked it. "You've never taken any of this seriously, Michael. You've always treated this like a game. Maybe it's because you're not German. But this isn't a game. It's real."

It was strange, hearing the things I'd just been saying to myself come from Fritz's lips. It was as though I suddenly stepped outside myself and saw me sitting there on the ground at Fritz's feet. We were just thirteen, me and Fritz, but we didn't look like boys anymore. Nazi Germany, the war, the Hitler Youth — all of it had made us into men. Not "man-gods" as Hitler had said, but boy-men. Boys whose insides, whose hearts and minds and souls, had been forced to grow up faster than our bodies. The war had made us men, and it was time to act like it.

"My parents are spies," I said.

ALL IN

I FELT LIGHT-HEADED AS I SAID IT. HOLLOW. LIKE IT WAS some dream version of me. Something that would go away when I woke up.

Fritz froze. *"What?"*

I wet my dry lips. "You're right. It's time for me to stop playing games. To commit myself completely. It's time I told the truth. *My parents are spies.* They're harboring the British airman. The one we were searching for in the countryside. They're hiding him until they can get him out of the country."

Fritz staggered back, the black smoke from the burning books swirling around him.

"Where?"

"I don't know," I lied. "But they're moving him tonight. You have to tell the Gestapo. I'll find out where and when, and lead them there."

Fritz blinked in amazement. His eyes went elsewhere as he considered all this, then finally found my face. When they did, the anger was gone, replaced by something like . . . admiration. Awe. He offered me his hand to help me up, and I took it. We were friends again, and I was the boy who'd denounced his parents to the Nazis.

There was only one thing left to do.

HOW TO TAKE A BEATING, PART 2

I CAUGHT HORST LATER THAT DAY COMING HOME FROM the over-age movie he'd snuck in to see at the cinema. I knew I could beat Horst in a fair fight, but this wasn't going to be a fair fight.

I hurried up behind him, threw a flour sack over his head, and kicked him in the back of the knee. He went down hard on the sidewalk, and before he could tear the sack off his head and see who attacked him, I kicked him hard, right in the ribs. I heard something crack, and he screamed and doubled over. A quick German Look told me we were still alone, and I kicked him again and again—his arms, his legs, his chest, his head. He'd had this coming ever since he'd been our Jungvolk leader, ever since he'd let the bigger boys pound the smaller boys for fun, ever since he'd put me and Fritz in the ring together and told him to keep getting up, ever since he'd beaten that Edelweiss Pirate to within an inch of his life. I gave Horst the beatdown he'd delivered to so many other boys, the beatdown I wanted the Allies to give to that bully Adolf Hitler. I kicked him and kicked him and kicked him until he didn't scream anymore, didn't moan, didn't move. He was still alive when I was finished, but just barely.

I dipped two fingers in the blood that was pooling on the sidewalk underneath him, and on the wall above his broken body I drew a picture of an edelweiss.

TONIGHT

I LED MY PARENTS INTO DA'S STUDY WHEN I GOT HOME and pulled Simon out of the hidden room.

"We have to do it tonight," I told them. This time my voice didn't crack. "There's been an opening on the science team."

OWLS IN THE NIGHT

IT WAS COLDER THAT NIGHT, AS IF WINTER HAD GIVEN spring a thrashing that would lay it up in the hospital for another month. I stamped my feet and buried my hands in the heavy over-coat I wore. It was even colder by the River Spree, on the pedestrian path underneath the Moltke Bridge. There were no *Fussgängers* down here tonight. No "footgoers." Not officially. It was after curfew. Everyone but the SRD and the Gestapo were supposed to be shut up tight in their homes.

A dozen of us waited in the shadows. Owls in the night, wait-ing for our prey to emerge. Our steamy breaths made faint gray clouds in the darkness.

"Where's Horst?" I whispered to Fritz. Ottmar and Erhard had been there when we set out from the Gestapo station, but not the fourth musketeer.

"The Pirates got him," Fritz growled.

I nodded. Not that Fritz or anyone else could see me, which let me smile a little in the darkness. The smile quickly faded, though.

I was far too nervous about what was about to happen to enjoy my easy victory over donkey-faced Horst.

We heard a soft step on the cement path under the bridge, and the breathing around me stopped as we all strained our ears to listen. A whisper — words I couldn't understand. The sound of scuffling feet. Whoever it was, they were coming our way. The wait was agonizing. My stomach did somersaults. Was this Simon? Or had we unwittingly scheduled this little piece of theater in the same place and on the same night that some family was trying to escape, some Edelweiss Pirates were attempting an act of vandalism? And if it *was* Simon, would the SS shoot first and ask questions later? Would he be sent to a concentration camp? What if the nervous sweat rolling down my back made the tape around my waist come loose, and the blueprints for Projekt 1065 slipped out of my shirt? What if the Nazis still didn't pick me for the team after I'd turned Simon and my parents in?

A flashlight clicked on, catching Simon full in the face. He looked genuinely startled. He flinched as if to run, but another flashlight clicked on, and another, and Simon blinked and raised his hands against the light that held him in place. It was obvious there were too many of us for him to run away.

Simon was caught.

KNOWING WHAT'S TO COME

"WHERE ARE YOUR PARENTS?" SS-OBERSTURMFÜHRER Trumbauer asked me.

"I — I don't know. They were supposed to be with him," I said, giving the answer my mother and father had prepared for me.

"The embassy — go. Go!" Trumbauer said, dispatching some of his soldiers. "Find them!"

I held my breath as the soldiers ran off into the night. I prayed my parents wouldn't be caught. They should already have been gone from the city hours ago, but it was a long way from Berlin to Dublin, and they would have very few allies along the way.

SS-Obersturmführer Trumbauer walked up close to Simon, who was being held by two SS men. Simon wasn't squirming or trying to get away.

"You should know, it was the O'Shaunesseys' son who turned you in. Turned his parents in too," Trumbauer said with unmitigated delight. It wasn't enough that he'd caught Simon. He wanted to rub my betrayal in his face.

"Michael?" Simon said, searching the darkness. "Michael, say it isn't so!"

The heartbreak in his voice was so real I thought my own heart would explode. How could anybody do this to someone else?

But I had a part to play, or else this would all be for nothing. I pushed through the other SRD boys in the darkness and stepped into the light.

"You're an enemy of the state," I told Simon, my voice shaky. "And my parents broke the laws of Germany hiding you. But even worse, they broke the laws of human nature. They betrayed the Aryan race by hiding a *Jew*." I said the word like an insult. Like profanity.

"How can you say that?" Simon asked. "How can you believe any of it?"

I stood taller, making sure the flashlights caught my puffed-up chest, my upturned chin. "Because I belong to Hitler now."

"I can see that you do," Simon said. "Well, if you belong to Hitler, why don't you go to him? *Go to the devil!*"

One of the soldiers slammed the stock of his rifle into Simon's stomach, and Simon doubled over in pain. I had to resist crying out for the soldier to stop, and did my best to hold back my tears. The boy in me was scared for what was going to happen to Simon now, scared to be on my own for the very first time in my life. I took a deep breath and tried to remember to be a man.

"I wonder, Michael," Simon said, still hunched over in pain, "did you ever hear the one about the Englishman, the Irishman, and the Scotsman who were all lined up in front of a firing squad?"

247

I couldn't believe Simon was telling jokes here, now. I didn't even have a chance to stammer a response before he went on.

"The lads are told they each can have a final request. The Scotsman says, 'I'd like to hear "Scotland the Brave" played on the bagpipes before I'm shot, to remind me of the auld country,' and the Irishman says, 'I'd like to hear "Danny Boy" sung by Gracie Fields before I'm shot, to remind me of the auld country.' So knowing what's to come, the Englishman says, 'I'd like to be shot first.'"

Simon yanked himself free, decked the closest SS man, and sprinted down the tunnel. Whistles blew. People shouted. Shots rang out. Simon fell. *No!* Without thinking, I ran to him, but luckily, others did too. One of the SS was already kneeling down beside him when I got there.

"He's dead," he said.

ANYTHING AND EVERYTHING

"HE DIED WHILE TRYING TO ESCAPE."

There was almost happiness in SS-Obersturmführer Trumbauer's voice as he said it. One more dead Jew—and an enemy soldier to boot.

No sucker punch, no broken bone had ever hurt so much as this. My knees went weak, like I was up on the rooftop with Simon all over again, the bombs exploding all around us. It was all I could do to stay on my feet, to not double over and sob like a baby. I couldn't keep the tears from streaming down my face, though, and I turned away so no one would see.

Simon had meant to do this all along, I realized. As soon as he'd suggested I turn him in, he'd planned to get shot. To die trying to escape rather than be taken alive by the Nazis. He knew what was to come, even if he pretended it didn't matter. If they took him alive, they would torture him, and eventually he'd tell them about stealing the plans for Projekt 1065. Maybe even tell them about me, and how I had helped him.

He'd died to protect me, to protect his mission. Committed suicide by Nazi. Now they couldn't torture Simon Cohen, and he couldn't reveal any secrets. Because Simon Cohen was dead.

"Why do you cry?" SS-Obersturmführer Trumbauer asked, shining his light in my face. I hurriedly wiped away my tears.

"I—I can't believe my parents threw their lives away for this filth," I said, thinking fast. "I can't believe they didn't see that he who serves the Führer serves Germany, and whoever serves Germany serves God."

It was Nazi claptrap propaganda, but SS-Obersturmführer Trumbauer nodded with approval. He put a comforting hand on my shoulder. It was all I could do not to flinch away from it.

"You have done well, Michael," SS-Obersturmführer Trumbauer told me. "Very well. You have done more for Hitler tonight than most men twice your age." He called Fritz and Ottmar and Erhard over with a flick of his head, and I tried not to watch as Simon's body was dragged away by the others.

"In fact," SS-Obersturmführer Trumbauer said, "I am in charge of training a select group of young men such as yourself for a very special mission for the Führer, and we have an open position on the team." He nodded at Fritz. "Quex here has suggested you for the job, and I quite agree with his recommendation."

Fritz smiled. I would have too if I hadn't just watched Simon gunned down in cold blood. I thought of my parents, somewhere out there in the cold, dark night, on the run from the Nazis. At least it all hadn't been for nothing.

"I would give anything and everything to be on that team," I told SS-Obersturmführer Trumbauer.

And I already had.

8,422 FEET

THE CABLE CAR BUMPED AND JUDDERED AS IT WENT over one of the pylons that supported it during its four-thousand-foot climb. I closed my eyes and gripped the metal bench so hard it left deep lines in my skin. I felt light-headed, and not just because of the thin air of the Swiss Alps.

Standing at the base of the aerial tramway in Mürren, I had watched the tiny little cable cars as they moved up and down the mountain, hanging from spiderweb-thin cables that snaked up into the snowcapped peaks above us. Now I was inside one of those little trams, dangling a hundred feet over a sea of green fir trees and white snow. Not that I was looking out the window.

"I think I can see my house from here!" Ottmar said. He and Erhard both ran back and forth across the cabin, weaving between the other passengers for the best views. I wished they would just sit still. Every time they moved from one side to the other, I could feel the cabin sway left to right, right to left.

"Is your friend going to be all right?" a woman asked Fritz, who sat beside me. "He looks a little green."

"Something he ate," Fritz said. All this time, and he was still covering for me, still helping me hide the fact that I was deathly afraid of heights. I was better with heights now than I ever had been—able to actually step onto a cable car I knew was about to climb up the second half of an 8,422-foot-tall mountain, for example—but only because of the work I'd done with Simon.

Simon. Whenever I closed my eyes, all I could see was him looking up at me. Punching an SS officer. Running. Twisting as the bullets hit him. Falling. I saw it play out in my head over and over again, like a piece of broken film. *Why did you have to do it, Simon?* Surely there had to have been some other way.

I wrenched my eyes open. The brilliant blue of the Alpine sky glared back at me through the windows—so many windows!—and I quickly stared at the floor.

I had to ignore what I knew lay just outside the walls and floor of the cabin. Space. Empty air.

Nothing.

An Irishman, a Scotsman, and an Englishman apply for a chauffeur's job, I thought, trying to distract myself, remembering Simon. *"I'm such a good driver, I can go within six inches of a cliff and not drive off,"* says the Scotsman. *"I'm such a good driver, I can go within one inch of a cliff and not drive off,"* says the Englishman. *"Oh yeah?" says the Irishman. "Well, I'm such a good driver I stay as far away from cliffs as I can."*

The long arm atop the cable car rumbled across another pylon, and I put a hand to my mouth for fear I'd puke all over the lady standing in front of us.

"That which doesn't destroy us makes us stronger," Fritz said, quoting an old German philosopher the Nazis loved. The last thing I needed right now was Nazi platitudes, but I nodded. I had to keep playing the part of the zealous Hitler Youth. For a little while longer, anyway.

"There it is!" someone said at last. "The resort!"

THE WAITING SNAKE

THE EDELWEISS RESORT CLUNG TO THE SIDE OF A MOUN-
tain a few hundred feet below the peak, its spindly-looking
wooden pillars supporting decks that stuck out into the air. It
was all golden-brown wood and soft glowing lights and pointy
A-frame roofs, covered with windows and terraces that offered
guests incredible sweeping long-distance views of the valley far
below.

Basically, it was an acrophobe's worst nightmare.

My legs wobbled as I left the cable car, but I was glad to be back
on solid ground. Even if that solid ground was eight thousand feet
in the air. I kept my back to the view and my eyes on the resort,
where all the passengers were queuing up in a *Warteschlange* — a
"waiting snake," German for a long line — to go through security.

Security! The Swiss soldiers at the doors were going through
the bags of each of the attendees and patting each of them down.
For weapons, I guessed, though one man in the full-dress

uniform of a country I didn't recognize was let through with the sword on his belt. They were searching for guns, then. Guns and explosives.

I glanced at Fritz and the other two boys. Each of us carried two cases — one with our clothes, and another with the scientific equipment to assemble our fake science projects. To attend the conference, we were posing as junior scientists, and the kits were our cover. I had no idea what the plan was. How we were supposed to assassinate Professor Goldsmit. Only Ottmar knew the plan, which he promised he would tell us when we got to the resort. Did he carry a rifle in his second suitcase? A bomb?

If the Swiss Guards at the door discovered the weapon we were to use to kill Professor Goldsmit, if they caught us and sent us back to Germany with our tails between our legs, then my job would be done for me. My parents, Simon, they would have sacrificed themselves for nothing. But the professor would be safe, and that's what mattered now.

What I was worried about were the plans for Projekt 1065 taped around my stomach.

One simple pat to the side of my body and the guards would feel the tape there. Open my shirt. Reveal the jet fighter plans I was still carrying. They might not care that I was hiding papers on my body, but Ottmar and Erhard and Fritz would care. I would never leave this resort with the plans — if I left the resort alive at all.

The waiting snake slithered closer to the Swiss Guards at the door, and the plans felt like a stone hanging around my waist.

I had to get rid of the papers before we went through security. Put them somewhere safe, where I could retrieve them on the way out.

A low stone wall separated the aerial tramway station from the small plaza where we waited. That cable car was the only way out of the resort. The only way down the mountain.

"I'll be right back," I told Fritz, Ottmar, and Erhard. I broke away from the line and went behind the low wall. I felt along it for a loose stone and finally found one about the right size. I would hide the plans here, in the stone wall, where they would be safe from snow and Nazi assassins and Swiss Guards, then come back for them on the way to the cable car when I was leaving.

I had to duck not to be seen over the low wall. I unbuttoned my shirt enough to reach inside, and undid the medical tape Ma had given me to strap the plans to my skin. At last they were free, and I pulled out the thick packet of papers.

"What are you doing?" a voice asked.

A THOROUGH SECURITY CHECK

I WAS SO SURPRISED I NEARLY JUMPED OFF THE MOUN-
tain. It was Fritz! He was staring down at me from the other side
of the wall. I hastily stuffed the jet plans back inside my shirt and
kept my hand there, bent double to hide them. Had Fritz seen me
pull them out?

"I—I still feel sick from the cable car ride," I told Fritz. Which
was truer than I wanted to admit. "I just—I came back here in case
I needed to throw up. So the others wouldn't see. Will you cover
for me?"

"Of course," Fritz said. "Take whatever time you need."

Fritz disappeared, and I let out the breath I'd been holding. My
heart was still racing from the scare, and my fingers fumbled the
packet as I withdrew it again. I pulled the stone from the wall,
worked the plans as far inside the hole as I could, and wedged the
stone back into place. It stuck a few inches out from the wall,
making it pretty easy to find again.

I came back to Fritz, Ottmar, and Erhard just as they reached the Swiss Guards at the door. The Swiss wore gray uniforms with red collars signifying their rank, but where other countries would use stars, the little pips were shaped like edelweiss.

"You're fine to go through," the Swiss Guard at the door said, waving us inside without checking our bags or patting us down. I couldn't believe it. They were just going to let us through? Because we were *children*? It was just like Ma had told me: *Women and children make terrific spies, because people always underestimate us.* So this was why the Nazis sent boys to do the work of men. Did no one else have any idea what monsters the Hitler Youth were? What we were capable of? What we had been training to do since we were ten? They didn't even take our daggers from us!

"Wait, you're not going to — " I started to say, but Ottmar pulled me through the door with the rest of them, and we were inside.

Fritz murmured something to Ottmar, who nodded and sent Fritz on some assignment. I looked around for another Swiss soldier. They were all over the resort. I had to get word to one of them. Let them know what was happening. Then they could search our bags and see why the team had been sent. I headed for a blond guard in the lobby.

Ottmar grabbed my shirt and pulled me back. "No wandering," he said. "Let's get to our room. It's time to set up our 'experiment.'"

THE SCIENCE EXPERIMENT

OTTMAR EMPTIED THE CONTENTS OF HIS SUITCASE OUT on one of the beds in our room. I scanned the equipment, looking for a gun, a bomb, anything, but it was only a random collection of scientific equipment, just like mine. I frowned.

"Empty the others," Ottmar told us.

Erhard and I overturned the scientific suitcases onto the bed. It was a *Kuddelmuddel*. There was nothing dangerous or suspicious in it that I could see.

"Find the pieces with the red dots," Ottmar told us. He held one up to show us the little red dot painted on it.

Fritz came back from whatever errand he'd been sent on, gave Ottmar a cryptic nod, and then the four of us sifted through the equipment until we found all the ones with red dots and separated them out. Ottmar swept all the other equipment off the bed with a theatrical clatter. With practiced skill, he quickly assembled the pieces with the red dots into one whole that fit exactly into one of the four scientific suitcases.

"*A bomb*," Fritz said.

It *was* a bomb. It was obvious now. Wires, battery, a timer, and what looked like enough explosives to blow the top off the mountain. Ottmar smiled.

"Gentlemen, I give you our science project."

Even if the Swiss soldiers had searched our suitcases, they would never have found the bomb. It had been split up into pieces and hidden among the random useless equipment in our four suitcases. This was why they needed four of us, and why nothing else mattered but our fervent devotion to the Führer. We were nothing but four loyal mules, our suitcases packed with death.

Nazi Germany's chief export.

Ottmar snapped the latches closed on the suitcase bomb, and replaced it on the bed with one of the other empty scientific suitcases.

"Quickly now," he told us. "The civilian clothes from your suitcases, your papers, your money, only what you'll need for the trip home. Pack them together in here."

This was part of the plan we had at least all been briefed on — our escape. Once the deed was done, we were to descend the mountain and make our way by train to the border, posing as four Swiss boys on holiday. We had fake passports and everything. The border guards would be waiting to let us back into Germany, where we would be received with a hero's welcome. On the train from Berlin, Ottmar and Erhard had talked endlessly about what medals we would receive. The medals would be more impressive, they reasoned, if we lost an arm or a leg on our mission.

I would have to see what I could do to help them achieve that goal, at least.

When the other suitcase was packed, Ottmar snapped it closed and set it next to the one with the bomb.

"Erhard and I will plant the bomb. The detonator is preset to fifteen minutes," Ottmar told us. "Quex, you and Michael will go to the front desk and tell them you see a crack in the snowpack above the resort. The resort administrators will then sound the avalanche alarm, at which point the guests will be herded into the safety of the hotel's basement deep inside the mountain. That is where the bomb will be set. Fifteen minutes later, the bomb will detonate and everyone inside will be killed."

"Everybody?" I said. "I thought we were just here to kill Professor Goldsmit."

Ottmar shrugged. "What do a few more dead scientists matter? None of them are German." Ottmar checked his watch, then handed Fritz a suitcase. "You will carry the suitcase for our escape. You must hurry when you go to the front desk. Once the bomb is activated, it cannot be turned off. You must sound the alarm at *precisely* the same moment we turn on the timer. That will give the hotel staff just enough time to get everyone to the basement before the bomb goes off. We will meet you at the cable car and ride back down together. Synchronize watches."

"Wait, we're doing this *now*?" I said. I panicked. I had thought I'd at least have a chance to approach a guard during the conference, let them know what the plan was.

Ottmar picked up the suitcase with the bomb in it. "Goldsmit is already here. Quex saw him in the lobby." So that's what Fritz's mission had been—find Goldsmit. "There is no reason to wait," Ottmar said. He patted the suitcase. "We will do our job, and be well on our way home to our reward when our science project here goes off."

My heart was thumping so hard I was sure the other boys could hear it. My eyes flicked from the suitcase bomb to Ottmar to Erhard to Fritz. I could beat each of them in a straight fight, but not all together. Not all at once. Not here. How was I going to stop them?

"We go now," Ottmar said. "For Hitler!"

"For Hitler!" the other boys cried.

And the mission to assassinate Professor Hendrik Goldsmit began before I could stop it.

COMING CLEAN

OTTMAR AND ERHARD RAN ONE WAY DOWN THE HALL, and Fritz and I ran the other. Fritz carried the suitcase with our clothes in it.

"Fritz, we can't do this!" I told him. "Dozens of innocent people will be killed. Hundreds!"

"Hundreds of innocent people are killed all over Germany each night when the bombs fall," Fritz said. "This is no different."

There was no changing his mind. No changing any of their minds.

Fritz turned a corner. Instead of following him, I pulled up short and sprinted in the other direction, looking for a Swiss soldier. If Fritz noticed I wasn't behind him, he wouldn't stop. He had a schedule to keep.

It felt like forever but was probably just a minute or two before I found a Swiss soldier. I ran up to him, out of breath, and hurriedly tried to explain. "The boys I came with — they have a bomb! They're going to—to blow up the resort! You have to stop them!"

It took another agonizingly long few minutes for the Swiss Guard to confer with his lieutenant, and for me to explain all over again.

"It's in a suitcase. Two boys have it," I told them. "I can show you where!"

Finally, the soldiers let me lead them down the stairs to the basement. We caught Ottmar and Erhard looking for a place to hide the suitcase among the stacked-up chairs and tables and storage crates. Ottmar still had it in his hands.

"There. That's it," I told the soldiers. "The bomb's in that suit-case." I was exposing myself now. Letting Ottmar and Erhard know I was a traitor in their midst. But it didn't matter. It was all going to be over soon. It was time to come clean.

The soldiers pointed rifles at the boys, and Ottmar and Erhard held up their hands. The Swiss lieutenant took the suitcase from them, set it gently on the floor, and flipped the latches. I flinched, worried the bomb might go off before its timer. The Swiss soldier lifted the lid slowly, carefully, and we all saw what was inside—

A messy pile of clothing.

A SILLY PRANK

THE BOMB WASN'T IN THE SUITCASE.

I shook my head and took a step back. But — no. I had watched Ottmar put the bomb in the suitcase. I'd seen him pick it up and take it with him! Had they doubled back and picked up one of the others? No, there wouldn't have been time. We'd left the room together, each of our teams with a suitcase —

Understanding hit me like an avalanche. *Fritz*. Fritz and I had carried the suitcase with the bomb, not Ottmar and Erhard. They'd known all along I was a traitor. They'd tricked me into revealing my hand. And now Fritz was somewhere loose in the hotel with the bomb.

Ottmar looked innocent. "I don't know what this is all about," he told the soldiers. "Michael told us our rooms were in the basement, but there don't appear to be any guest rooms down here."

The Swiss lieutenant frowned at me. "A joke, then. Is that what this is? A silly prank? Send your friends down here looking for their room and then drag us after them, telling us they're carrying a bomb?"

"*A bomb?*" Erhard said. He looked at me in horror. "Michael, a joke is a joke, but telling them we're carrying a bomb — and with a war going on, no less!"

"No," I told the soldiers. "They're lying. You don't understand — "

"We take bomb threats very seriously in this country," the lieutenant told me. He took me by the arm. "There are penalties for making false alarms."

As if on cue, alarm bells rang throughout the resort. The Swiss soldiers looked up in a panic.

"The avalanche warning!" one of them said.

"No, wait!" I told them. "This was part of the plan! It's a distraction!"

The lieutenant ignored me. Avalanche alarms trumped boys who cried wolf any day. "Stay here," he told us. "Don't leave this room! You're safe in this room!"

The Swiss soldiers ran from the room, and suddenly I was alone with Ottmar and Erhard. Ottmar smiled wolfishly at me. Erhard cracked his knuckles.

Ottmar took a step toward me, fists clenched. "You heard what the man said, Michael. Don't leave the room. You're *safe* here."

PROFESSOR HENDRIK GOLDSMIT

I RAN FOR THE DOOR, BUT ONE OF THEM GRABBED ME BY the shirt and yanked me back. Ottmar? Erhard? I swung as I turned, my fist glancing off somebody's cheekbone in the same moment one of them kicked me in the shin. Pain flared through me like a firebomb, but I couldn't think about it. A fist found my stomach, doubling me over, a knee found my face, knocking me back. I slammed into a stack of chairs three times as tall as me, the tower of seats swaying precariously as I clung to it, trying to stay on my feet. And suddenly I was back in that school yard in London again, remembering that if you fell down, it was over.

I wiped my dripping nose. Ottmar and Erhard grinned like hyenas and converged on me. Rage coursed through my veins. If Hitler wanted his youth to learn how to take a beating, I would give these two boys their final lesson. The same lesson I'd taught to Horst.

No. No, I don't have time for this. The alarm was still going off. Any minute now, people would start flooding into this room, hiding out from an avalanche that wasn't coming. Fritz still had the suitcase bomb. He was the one I had to find, the one I had to stop.

But Ottmar and Erhard were standing in the way.

I grabbed the swaying stack of chairs behind me and pulled. The tower came crashing down on the boys, knocking them aside. I bolted for the door and ran for the stairs. Guests were already streaming down them. They weren't stampeding, but they were moving quickly. Men in suits and ties, women in nice dresses. Scientists and thinkers from around the Western world. I couldn't let these people die.

The top of the stairs was crowded, and I was running the wrong way. A soldier tried to turn me around, but I slipped under his arms and charged ahead, running straight into a short, thin man with curly black hair and round glasses.

"Professor Goldsmit?" I said. I recognized him from a photograph the science team had been shown. "Are you Professor Hendrik Goldsmit?"

"I—yes," he said, surprised to be recognized. The current of people took us back toward the stairs.

"Professor Goldsmit! You have to come with me!" I told him. I tried to pull him away.

"No. But the alarms—the avalanche," he said, pulling me with him. We had each other by the arms, each tugging in the opposite direction.

"You can't go down there," I told him. "Your life is in danger! A group of boys have been sent from Germany to kill you!"

A few of the people streaming around us for the basement turned to look at us when they heard that, but they didn't stop.

"Kill me? But how? Why?"

"Because of your work—" I leaned in close and lowered my voice. *"Because of your work on the atomic bomb."*

Professor Goldsmit's eyes went wide. He pulled me out of the flow of traffic over to the wall, where we had a bit more privacy.

"But—but—how can you know that?"

"Because the Nazis know it!" I told him. Gah! This was taking too long! "Look at me. Look at this uniform. I was on the team sent to kill you, but I'm Irish." I switched to speaking English. "I'm a spy for the Allies! I was sent here to save you!"

Goldsmit let me pull him along away from the basement as he struggled to understand. "But—you're just a boy!"

"My father is the Irish ambassador to Germany," I told him. *"Was* the Irish ambassador. We found out too late to tell anyone else. They had to send me."

"But this is—this is incredible!" Goldsmit stopped in an empty hallway next to a table with a vase full of edelweiss flowers. "Switzerland is neutral!"

"Do you think the Nazis care?" I asked him.

As if to prove my point, Ottmar jumped us from behind.

DREAMS OF MEDALS

OTTMAR THREW HIMSELF AT GOLDSMIT WITH A ROAR. HE drove the professor into the table, knocking him and the vase to the carpet. Ottmar raised his dagger to plunge it into Goldsmit's heart, but I tackled him first. We tumbled head over heels, kicking and punching and scrabbling for control of his dagger. Ottmar ended up on top of me, his dagger pointed at my throat. I pushed back with one hand and groped beside me with the other. I felt the knife tip nick my throat, felt the warm trickle of blood run down the side of my neck, and then my free hand found it—the flower vase. I whipped it up into the side of Ottmar's head, shattering it. It rang with a high, hollow clang like a church bell, and Ottmar crashed into the wall, unconscious. It wasn't a lost limb, but maybe there was a medal you could get for brain damage.

Professor Goldsmit helped me to my feet and gave me a handkerchief to stop the bleeding on my neck. "Do you believe me now?" I asked him.

He nodded emphatically. I grabbed his arm and pulled him along. Forget Fritz and the bomb. If I could get Goldsmit out of here, Fritz wouldn't blow the place up. Not when Erhard told him Goldsmit wasn't in the basement. Goldsmit was the mission. They could blow this resort to kingdom come, but they couldn't come back to Germany if they didn't blow up Goldsmit with it.

"Wait!" Goldsmit said, pulling me to a stop.

"*What now?*"

"We have to find Otto Strassmann," Goldsmit said. "He's an Austrian physicist. He's why I'm here. I'm supposed to recruit him for the Manhattan Project, and take him with me back to the United States!"

I couldn't believe this guy. "Did you not see Ottmar try to kill you just now? Who's more important, you or this Strassmann guy?"

Goldsmit straightened his glasses. "Well, Strassmann's done excellent work on the thermodynamics of superconductors, but *I* was the one who first proposed the idea of electron spin—"

I had no idea what he was talking about. "You win," I told him. "You can try and recruit him another time, when somebody *isn't* trying to kill you." I grabbed Goldsmit by the sleeve and pulled him along.

I kept my eyes peeled for Fritz as we ran for the lobby of the resort, but he wasn't anywhere. I hauled Goldsmit out the front door and headed for the cable car.

Goldsmit looked worriedly up at the snowcapped mountain behind the resort. "But what about the avalanche?"

"There isn't an avalanche," I told him. "That was just to get everybody into the basement so they could blow you up with a bomb!"

"Good God," Goldsmit said.

"Yeah," I said. "Wait here." I ran for the place where I'd tucked the plans for Projekt 1065. I was getting out of here with Goldsmit *and* the jet fighter plans. I was going to get more medals than Ottmar and Erhard could even dream about.

I was just imagining Winston Churchill, the British prime minister, pinning the Victoria Cross on my shirt when I pulled the stone from the wall and froze.

The Projekt 1065 plans were gone.

MAD AS HELL

THE HOLE WAS EMPTY.

I checked again. Had I found the wrong stone? No. This was the right place. This was the right stone.

The jet fighter plans were gone. But how? If the stone had fallen out and the plans had blown away, the stone would be on the ground, not stuck back in the hole. Which meant someone had come along behind me, pulled out the stone, taken the plans, and put the stone back where I'd left it. And there was only one person I could think of who'd done it.

Fritz.

He *had* seen me pull the plans out of my shirt. *That's* what he'd been talking to Ottmar about in the lobby of the resort. Ottmar might have sent him out to look for Goldsmit, but he'd also sent him to see what I'd stuck in the wall. My heart sank. They'd known since we left our hotel room that I was a traitor. That's how Ottmar had known to switch suitcases. To send the bomb with Fritz. They knew I'd lose Fritz as soon as I could and run to tell on Ottmar and Erhard, while Fritz ran free to finish the assassination.

An icy chill swept through me. Fritz knew I'd betrayed him. Not just today, but all along. When he looked at what I'd hidden in the wall, he would have known at once what they were. He would know why I'd come over to his house all those times, why I'd joined the SRD with him, why I'd pretended to be his friend. He would know it was all to steal the jet fighter plans out from under his nose and hand them over to the Allies.

Fritz was still out there with the bomb, and he was mad as hell.

"We have to get out of here," I told Goldsmit, pushing him toward the cable car station. "*Now.*"

Another tram was just reaching the station. A few people were on it, and we pushed past them to get on board. I caught a glimpse of the long, long drop down the mountainside as I put Goldsmit in a seat, and I almost blacked out right then and there. It was only the adrenaline coursing through my system that kept me awake. I grabbed for one of the hand straps that hung from the ceiling and wrapped myself around one of the poles. I wanted to close my eyes, to sink to the floor and pass out, but I couldn't. Fritz might come running for the tram any second now, suitcase bomb in hand. I had to protect Goldsmit. Had to get him to safety. Eyes fluttering, I unsnapped the Hitler Youth dagger on my belt and hugged the pole, willing myself to stay awake, to stay on my feet.

When you fell down, it was over.

"Did you hear the one about the Englishman, the Irishman, and the Scotsman who were all staying at the world's tallest hotel?" I asked Goldsmit without turning around.

"Um, no. I can't say I have," Goldsmit said.

The glass doors to the tram slid shut, and the cable car moved away from the station. We'd made it. "I'll tell you later," I said, and I gave in and slumped to the ground at last.

Something big and heavy thumped on the roof of the cable car, and I jerked awake. The metal blade of a dagger was sticking through the roof, keeping whoever had jabbed it there from sliding off the top of the car. The dagger had words on it. From where I sat, pooled helplessly on the floor, I could read them:

BLOOD AND HONOR!

Fritz was on the roof of the cable car.

FOR THE GLORY
OF OLD IRELAND

A BROWN SUITCASE DIPPED BELOW THE EDGE OF THE roof. I could see it through the window. Fritz's head peeked through the window upside down. He saw me, saw Professor Goldsmit, and then he and the suitcase disappeared again.

Fritz was on the roof of the cable car, and he had the suitcase bomb.

He had waited for us. He knew I'd go for Professor Goldsmit and try to get him out of the resort. Fritz had waited for us on top of the cable car station, watched us get on board. Separated us from the others so he could kill us.

Professor Goldsmit stood and went to the window, trying to see up top. "What's going on? Who was that boy?"

"He's — he's one of the ones sent to kill you," I said. I closed my eyes and fought off my nausea. I wished Goldsmit would sit down. He was making the cabin rock. "His name is Fritz. He has a bomb."

"A bomb! But if he blows us up, he'll die too."

"He doesn't care," I told him. "He was born to die for Germany." I'd said it sarcastically, but I realized suddenly that it was true. Fritz believed all that stuff about sacrificing himself for the Fatherland. For Hitler. He would do it. He would fulfill the Hitler Youth motto: *Live faithfully, fight bravely, and die laughing.*

Goldsmit fretted around the cabin like a caged chicken. "But we're trapped in here! It's a forty-minute ride to the bottom!"

And the bomb had a fifteen-minute timer. I knew the score. We were in trouble.

We were going to die.

"We have to get up there!" Goldsmit said. "We have to stop him! He'll blow us all up!"

I nodded. He was right. But I couldn't be the one to do it.

Goldsmit didn't wait for me to help him. He tried the doors first, but those were locked tight, of course. They didn't want anybody accidentally opening them and falling to their death. He tried the windows next, and managed to get one of them open. He did all this while I lay curled around one of the poles in the middle of the cabin, fighting desperately not to black out.

"I opened a window, but I can't fit!" Goldsmit said. "You could, though."

I would have laughed if I wasn't afraid I would throw up. "I'll fall. I'll die," I told him.

"Young man, listen to me," Goldsmit said. "He has a bomb, and if he's as crazy as you say he is, he'll use it. One way or the other, you're going to die. We both are. Wouldn't you rather die fighting?"

"I'm such a good driver, I stay as far away from cliffs as I can," I told him, remembering my joke. Goldsmit didn't understand. But I knew Simon would. And I also knew Simon would be telling me to get up, to confront my fear. Simon had died fighting rather than be led quietly to his death, and he'd want me to do the same.

I pulled myself up the pole to my knees. I kept my eyes on the floor.

"Did you hear the one about the Englishman, the Irishman, the Scotsman, and the Welshman who were riding in a hot-air balloon?"

"I—no," Goldsmit said. "Is this really a time for jokes?"

I pulled myself to my feet. "The balloon was about to crash into a mountain," I went on. "So the pilot says to them, 'We need to lose more weight to get clear. One of you has to jump.'" I took a step across the cabin, going from one pole to the other. "So the Scotsman—the Scotsman, he says, 'I do this for the glory of Scotland!' and he jumps out of the basket." I let go of the pole and grabbed hold of the window. Goldsmit was right—it was just big enough for me to climb through.

Outside, a white-and-brown mountain peak sailed by. The tram rumbled as it went over one of the pylons that supported the cable, and I swallowed hard.

"But the balloon wasn't high enough yet. 'We need to lose more weight!' the pilot says. So the Welshman says, 'I do this for the glory of Wales!' and jumps out of the balloon to his death."

"I don't understand how any of this—" Goldsmit started to say, but I held up a hand to quiet him. I steadied my breathing and stepped up onto the bench below the window.

" 'We need to lose the weight of just one more person, and we'll make it!' the pilot says." I reached outside the window. Felt the cold mountain air humming by. Found a ledge on the roof to pull myself up on. "So the Irishman, he says, 'I do this for the glory of old Ireland!' and he picks up the Englishman and throws him over the side."

I looked back at Goldsmit. He was frowning as though he didn't understand.

"For the glory of old Ireland," I said, and I hauled myself up and out the window.

DON'T LOOK DOWN

WIND WHIPPED MY HAIR INTO MY FACE. THE METAL LEDGE
of the roof was cold and hard under my fingers. Bit into my skin. I
worked my feet onto the windowsill and raised my head. I couldn't
see the roof because I had my eyes squeezed shut. *I should probably open them at some point if I plan on actually climbing on top
of the cable car*, I realized. But right then, I was just fine with
them closed. I was just fine standing here on top of the window,
not looking.

But I didn't have time for this. Fritz was up there, with a bomb.
Did you hear the one about . . . did you hear the one about . . .

I couldn't do it. Couldn't focus. I lost control of my breathing,
started hyperventilating. If I didn't move soon, I was going to fall.
I was going to fall, and Fritz was going to blow Professor Goldsmit
into the atoms he liked to study.

*You have to open your eyes, Michael. There's no other way
to do it.*

I opened my eyes. All I saw was the white painted top of the aerial tram, curving up and away from me, blue sky beyond. Good. This was good. I could do this. I could do this. *Just don't look down,* I told myself. *Don't look down. Don't look down.*

I looked down.

Fir trees. Giant fir trees. And the tops of them were far below me. I could see all the way down them, all the way to the snowy forest floor.

The earth shrank away from me and came screaming at me at the same time. My brain detached from the rest of my body, floated away, and I was outside myself again, watching my body go slack, watching my hands let go, watching my feet slide off the windowsill.

Watching myself fall.

MIGHT MAKES RIGHT

A HAND GRABBED MINE. HELD ON LIKE A PIT BULL. PULLED me up over the edge, until I lay dazed and addled in the middle of the cable car's roof, Fritz panting beside me.

Fritz. Fritz had saved me from falling.

"That's two," Fritz said. Two times he had saved me from falling. Two times he had saved my life. "Why do I keep saving you?" Fritz asked me.

I wondered the same thing. The metal roof under me made my skin crawl. Or maybe it was how exposed I was up here on the roof, the wind a living thing that pushed at me, nudged me, trying to throw off my balance. Trying to push me over the side.

When you fell down, it was over.

I dragged myself to the arm that connected the center of the roof to the thick metal cables higher above us. It was too big to wrap my arms around, but I put my back to it, taking a little shelter from the wind.

Fritz stood in the middle of the roof, the wind pushing and pulling at his clothes. The suitcase lay on its side between his feet. He looked like Hitler's man-god up here, Zeus standing atop Mount Olympus, a lightning bolt in his hand. Right at this moment, Fritz ruled the world. The only world that mattered to the two of us.

"I'm impressed!" Fritz said. "I know how hard it was for you to do that! You're learning to overcome your fear! That's good!"

"That which doesn't destroy us—" I said, my voice weak, almost carried away on the wind.

"—makes us stronger! Yes!" Fritz said. The cable car rumbled past another pylon, and Fritz rode the lurching tram like an old sailor standing his ground in a storm. "You did that for me, Michael. You made me stronger. You taught me how to fight back. Maybe that's why I keep saving you. Because you saved me."

"Made you into a monster, you mean."

Fritz frowned. "Is the wolf a monster for eating the rabbit? Is the hawk a monster for eating the mouse? All life is struggle, Michael. He who wants to live should fight for himself. He who doesn't fight doesn't deserve to live."

"Might makes right," I said.

"Yes! Exactly!" Fritz said. "This is the law of nature. This is why Germany will win!"

Slowly, I felt myself coming back to life, felt my arms and legs and head as though they were all attached to my brain again, not separate things floating away from each other. My chest still heaved from the panic of falling, but it was settling down, slowing. I had to get control. I had to be here for this. As wrong as Fritz was about everything else, he was right about one thing: If I didn't fight for myself now, I wasn't going to live.

"Fritz—Fritz, listen to me. You're not a monster. I know it. That's why you separated us from the rest of the guests at the resort, so you wouldn't kill all those innocent people. You don't have to kill Professor Goldsmit. You don't have to kill me. You don't have to kill *yourself*. There's another way out of all this. You don't have to start that timer."

"Oh, I'm sorry, Michael. I don't think you understand," Fritz said. "I already did."

THE NEW MICHAEL

MY BODY SANK. IF FRITZ HAD ALREADY STARTED THE timer, we had only minutes left. Maybe seconds. How long ago had he turned it on? How long had it taken me to climb out that window? For him to pull me up on the roof? How long had I been lying here just *talking* to him? I had to *do* something!

"I should be mad at you, you know," Fritz said calmly, as if he hadn't just told me the bomb between his feet was ticking down to our deaths. He pulled a packet of papers from inside his shirt and held them up for me to see.

The plans for Projekt 1065.

"All that time, you weren't really my friend," Fritz said. "You were just using me."

"It was like that at first," I told him. "But I really did become your friend. I still am."

Fritz shook his head. "No, you're not my friend." He waved the jet fighter plans at me. "You're the enemy. And I beat you!"

Fritz ripped the packet of papers open and the wind tore them away. They disappeared over the side, lost forever in the Alpine forest below. All that work, gone with the wind. The gaping pit in my stomach grew wider. Now the Allies would never match the Germans in the air. The war would end before Goldsmit or anybody else could build an atomic bomb.

"I should be mad at you, but I'm not," Fritz said. "I respect you for what you did. You're fighting for what you believe in! There's honor in that, even if you're wrong."

"There's honor in kicking that suitcase over the side too," I told him. "There's honor in a fair fight, in not killing your enemies when they can't fight back. Not murdering them."

Fritz smiled and spread his arms wide, swaying a little in the wind. "If you want to kick this suitcase over the side, come do it."

He was teasing me. He knew I wouldn't do it. Knew I *couldn't* do it. He was just going to stand there taunting me until the bomb went off because my fear of heights had paralyzed me.

But that was the old Michael. The Michael who thought all this was a game.

This was the Michael who knew it was real.

I pulled myself up on the arm of the cable car, drew my Hitler Youth dagger from its sheath, and took a step toward him, ready to fight.

SHUNK

THE LOOK OF EASY VICTORY ON FRITZ'S FACE FALTERED.
He hadn't expected me to actually get up. He took a frightened
step back, then remembered we were on top of a cable car. He did
the German Look over his shoulder to get his bearings, planted
his feet again, and drew his dagger. With his other hand, he picked
up the suitcase with the bomb in it. He wasn't just going to let me
kick it off the roof. If I wanted to throw it over the side, I was
going to have to take it from him.

Fine. Then that's what I would do.

The tram rumbled onto another one of the support pylons, and
I used that moment to charge him. I swiped at him with my dagger. He jerked back out of the way and threw the suitcase in
between us like a shield. The suitcase was heavy, though, too
heavy to hold up for long. His arm dropped, and in the opening I
gave him a quick jab with my left fist, punching him square in the
nose. He staggered a step back and dropped his dagger. It rattled
across the rooftop and fell over the side.

Fritz's eyes filled with fear. I'd taught him how to fight, but he still wasn't good enough to beat *me*.

I lunged at him with the dagger. He threw the suitcase up again, holding it with both hands. *Shunk!* My dagger sank four inches into the suitcase, slicing right through the leather case and into the machinery inside.

We froze—me still holding the knife, Fritz still holding the suitcase—waiting for the bomb to explode.

IT DIDN'T.

THOOM

TIME UNFROZE. I YANKED THE KNIFE OUT, AND FRITZ reared back with the suitcase to knock me off my feet.

Fritz swung. I swung.

I ducked. Fritz didn't.

The dagger caught him in the arm, tearing a long gash through fabric and skin. Blood sprayed from the tip of my dagger as it cut clean through, and Fritz screamed and clapped a hand to his arm.

The hand that had been holding the suitcase.

It clattered to the roof, slid down the curve, and caught on the ledge.

Fritz and I gave each other the same startled look, then dove for the suitcase at the same time. We hit the roof with a thump, and the suitcase bounced over the side and plummeted into the snowpack far below.

"No. *No!*" Fritz screamed. He turned and started beating wildly on me with his fists the way he had that first day he'd fought back in the classroom, not really hurting me so much as disorienting me. I dropped my dagger, and Fritz snatched it up before it slid away. He climbed to his feet.

"I'll just climb down there and kill him myself!" Fritz told me. "You can come after me if you want. But this time I'm not going to save you when you fall!"

THOOM.

The suitcase bomb detonated far below us, the shock waves so strong I could feel them all the way up here. It didn't do anything but surprise us. Sober us.

Or so we thought.

At first it sounded like thunder, like the creaking of a metal swing on the playground. Then it turned into a low rumble, like a plane flying high overhead. And then ten planes. And then a hundred planes. And then a waterfall, a never-ending torrent. And then we saw what it was.

The explosion had triggered an avalanche.

AVALANCHE!

FRITZ AND I WATCHED, TRANSFIXED, AS SNOW ROARED down the side of the mountain toward the forest of fir trees below.

Toward us.

At first I couldn't believe it would possibly reach us, but as the snow rolled down the mountain, giant clouds of it blossomed and roiled, growing bigger and taller.

The avalanche was going to hit the cable car.

I rolled for the arm at the center of the roof, wrapping my whole body around it just as the first snow burst hit us. The snow stung like sleet, and then the bigger clouds caught us. Snow and rock slammed into me like gravel fired from a cannon. I heard Fritz cry out, but couldn't see him in the storm.

I clung to the arm of the cable car and held on as the tram was knocked sideways, sweeping up and away from the avalanche like a flag in the wind. The snow pummeled me, beat me like waves, trying to strip me free, but I held on.

And then it was past. The tidal wave of snow rumbled on down the mountain, the aerial tram swung sickeningly back down to how it was supposed to hang, and I sucked in a desperate lungful of air, snow and ice still covering every inch of my body.

I had hung on, but Fritz hadn't. I was alone on the roof of the cable car.

When you fell down, it was over.

UNTOUCHED BY WAR

THE TRAIN COMPARTMENT ROCKED LIKE THE CABLE CAR swinging in the sky, but this one was mercifully connected to the ground. I slumped heavily against the window, still stunned that I had been able to save Professor Goldsmit, who sat on the seat across from me. Still stunned that I had fought Fritz on top of a cable car. That I had watched him there, clinging to the roof of the gondola one moment, gone the next.

Goldsmit and I had caught a train from Mürren to Bern, the capital of Switzerland, where there was an Irish Embassy just like the one in Berlin. Only this one, presumably, still had an ambassador. Once I handed over Goldsmit, he wasn't my responsibility anymore.

Our train rumbled along the sweeping curve of a stone bridge, a lazy, crystal-blue river below us. Enormous evergreen trees stood like sentinels along hillsides covered in a soft white blanket of snow. A little village with peaked roofs, a church steeple, and smoking chimneys glowed yellow-orange in the fading twilight.

This was a Europe untouched by war. This was a Europe where no bombs had fallen, no Jews had been rounded up and sent to concentration camps, no tanks had torn the streets up with their treads. Where homes and churches and schools still stood, where food was plentiful, where people still greeted one another warmly on the sidewalk, without suspicion. This was Switzerland, protected from the horrors on their doorstep by the thin shield of neutrality, the paper wall of diplomacy and politics.

Just like Ireland.

But the war that was being fought just outside the borders of Switzerland and just across the Celtic Sea from Ireland wasn't just a war between the Axis and the Allies. It was a *world* war, and the fate of every nation on Earth, neutral or not, lay in the balance. When the war was over, the world would be ruled one way, or the other — by freedom or fascism, by hope or by fear. I had seen the depths, the lengths, the Nazis would go to win that war, sacrificing their own children to the cause, and I also knew firsthand the sacrifices the Allies had made to stop them.

I wonder, Michael, did you ever hear the one about the Englishman, the Irishman, and the Scotsman who were all lined up in front of a firing squad?

Whether they wanted them to or not, Simon and the Allies were fighting to save the world for Switzerland too. And Ireland. What right did the Swiss, the Irish, the Spanish — *anyone* — have to sit out the fight for the fate of the world when they too would live or die by the result?

"A good man died to save you," I said to Goldsmit, startling him. They were the first words either of us had spoken since we boarded the train, weary from our adventure. My voice sounded harder than I'd meant it to, like an accusation.

"I didn't ask him to," Goldsmit said defensively.

"Well, he did, whether you wanted him to or not."

"I—I'm sorry," Goldsmit said.

"Don't be sorry," I told him. "Just . . . make that bomb. Save the world. Do something that makes your life worth saving."

Goldsmit took off his glasses, cleaned them with his handkerchief, and put them back on. "I'll do my best," he said.

I stared out the window again, at the white mountains in the distance. I thought of Simon, and of my parents. Where were they right now? In a barn in Germany? Hiding beneath a bridge in Nazi-occupied France? Or had they gone north into Denmark, looking for a ferry to take them across the North Sea to England? Surely they hadn't gone east, toward the Russian front.

Wherever they were, I prayed they were safe, and that I would see them again soon.

Our train pulled in to Bern less than an hour later. The station agent gave us directions, and the professor and I made our way to the Irish Embassy. I spent more than a minute explaining to the lady at the front desk who Goldsmit and I were and why we were there, before I realized I was still speaking German and had to start all over again in English.

"Yes, yes, Michael!" the woman said. "You've been expected!"

"I have?" I asked. "*We* have? By whom?"

But the lady was already on the phone, excitedly reporting our arrival. I heard a familiar voice give a happy cry somewhere down the hall. And then my mother and father and I were running to meet each other, wrapping one another in one great Irish hug.

AN ENGLISHMAN, A SCOTSMAN, AND AN IRISHMAN

"THAT SHOULD BE THE LAST OF THEM, THEN," CHIEF Technician Ross of the Royal Air Force said in his Scottish brogue. He shuffled the papers into a single stack and put his pencil and eraser on top of them. The pencil was blue, and had VENUS ~ BLUE BAND ~ SUPERTHIN ~ 3561 ~ NO2 printed on it in white. The eraser said WH SMIT. I assumed it once said WH SMITH, but the second H had worn off.

"You've an absolutely incredible memory for detail," said Agent Faulkner. He was in the SOE—Special Operations Executive, Britain's secret war intelligence organization—and a ramrod English aristocrat to the core. He was probably Lord something-or-other outside the war, and had gone to university at Oxford or Cambridge. Or both. "I doubt even I could have reconstructed those plans from memory after all this time," he said.

After our happy reunion, my parents and I had flown under cover of night from Bern to London, where we were now. While my parents had spent the last three days being debriefed by the SOE and receiving their new orders from Dublin, I had worked with Chief Technician Ross to rebuild the plans for Projekt 1065 from memory, exactly the same way Simon and I had in the little secret room at the Irish Embassy. It hadn't been easy, but I'd already done it once in Berlin. Why couldn't I do it again here? Now if the Nazis did build their jet-powered *Flugzeug* — "fly thing," the German word for "airplane" — the Allies would have one to match them.

"Have you ever heard the one about the Englishman, the Irishman, and the Scotsman who sold their brains as transplants?" I asked Agent Faulkner.

The British Intelligence officer looked a little taken aback. He glanced at the Scottish engineer, who just shook his head and smiled.

"I'm afraid I haven't," said Agent Faulkner.

"Well, it turns out the Irishman's and the Scotsman's brains only sold for a hundred pounds, but the Englishman's sold for five thousand pounds. 'It just goes to prove,' said the Englishman, 'that Englishmen are much cleverer than Irishmen or Scotsmen.' 'No, it doesn't,' said the Irishman. 'It just means the Englishman's brain had never been used.'"

"Right," Agent Faulkner said, not quite sure what to do with that. Chief Technician Ross tried to hide a smile.

Agent Faulkner stood. "I think we're about finished here. Chief Technician?"

The Scotsman gave me an easy salute and collected the papers. "Cheers, lad."

I joked, but the whole reason I'd been able to remember the plans was down to Simon, my English friend. He was the one who'd helped me hone my memory, the one who'd played Kim's Game with me night after night. He was the reason too that I'd been able to save Professor Goldsmit from Fritz.

Fritz. I thought of him again, standing over me, that bloody Hitler Youth dagger in his hands, ready to die for Germany. He had, in the end. Like the Hitler Youth's motto, he'd lived faithfully and fought bravely. But he hadn't died laughing.

"I understand you and your family are off to Washington, D.C., now," Agent Faulkner said when Ross was gone.

I nodded. We were going to America! "It's a new posting for my father," I said. "He reckons it'll be safer there than in Berlin, and Ma is going to help the Yanks with their new intelligence service." I paused, then asked, "What about Professor Goldsmit? Is he back in the States working on the atomic bomb?"

Agent Faulkner cleared his throat. "I really couldn't say."

Of course not. Loose lips sink ships and all that.

"So when do I get to meet Mr. Churchill?" I asked.

Agent Faulkner looked bewildered. "Meet Mr. Churchill?"

"You know, to get my medal. Get my picture in all the papers."

Faulkner looked uncomfortable. "You and your family may yet get a commendation from His Majesty's government," Agent Faulkner said. "That's not for me to say. But Michael, you *do* understand that you can't say a word about any of this. Ever. To anyone."

I frowned. "What? What do you mean I can't tell anyone?"

Agent Faulkner sat back down across from me. "Michael, it's imperative that you tell no one about what you and your parents have done. Not one bit of it. If you go telling your story, it will be obvious that we've had Irish agents working under Hitler's nose the whole war. That we still *do* have Irish agents in the field."

"What's wrong with that?" I asked. "People *should* know."

"Michael, it's vital that we maintain the illusion of Ireland's neutrality. It may yet be valuable to us. I'm afraid everything you've seen and heard, everything you and your parents have done for the war effort, falls under the Official Secrets Act. You're forbidden from telling anyone what happened, under penalty of imprisonment."

I couldn't believe it. My mother and father had been sending valuable intelligence to the Allies for years. I had just risked my life—and theirs, and sacrificed *Simon's* life—to get the plans for Projekt 1065. To save Professor Goldsmit. And now we couldn't tell anybody about it?

"It's not fair," I told Faulkner.

"Welcome to the world of international espionage," Agent Faulkner said, and he got up to leave. He stopped and gave me a sympathetic look. "I'm afraid you'll just have to sleep well in the knowledge that you and your family have done your part to win the war."

I huffed. It wasn't enough. I wanted the world to know what I'd done. What Ma and Da had done.

But then I remembered riding on the train through Switzerland with Goldsmit, feeling bitter about Ireland's neutrality in the war. The truth was, Ireland *wasn't* sitting on the sidelines. We *had* done something. We were just fighting in a different way.

Even though nobody would ever know what I'd done, what my ma and da had done, what *Ireland* had done, we'd stood up to Hitler and the Nazis with the rest of the Allies.

We'd fought for freedom too.

AUTHOR'S NOTE

IN MODERN HISTORY, YOUNG PEOPLE WERE PERHAPS never used so much to fight a war as they were in Nazi Germany during World War II. At the beginning of the war, when things were going well for the Nazis, German children worked on the home front. Like their Allied counterparts in England and America and Russia, they were farmers, messengers, and air raid wardens. They collected raw materials in scrap drives. They put out fires and cleared debris after bombings. They worked in factories and hospitals and welfare agencies.

But after the disastrous Battle of Stalingrad in early 1943, in which the Nazis lost more than 285,000 men, Germany became desperate for new soldiers. By that summer, Nazi Germany was officially drafting boys as young as sixteen for active military duty. They were given guns, grenades, and rocket launchers, and sent to the front lines with little or no training. Tens of thousands of young German boys died fighting on the Russian front alone.

In one extraordinary case, the Nazis created a special, fully equipped tank division manned entirely by Hitler Youth between the ages of sixteen and eighteen, and tasked them with stopping the Allied advance in France after D-Day. Of the more than 20,000 boys in the unit, almost half died in the war.

In late 1944, when Germany's defeat was all but certain, Adolf Hitler ordered that every male between the ages of fifteen and sixty who was not already fighting must join in the defense of Germany. But in reality, boys — and girls — as young as eleven years old were recruited to fight. The boys were given rocket launchers and grenades and sent to attack Allied tanks; the girls were taught to operate antiaircraft guns and told to shoot down enemy planes. During the battle for the city of Aachen, American soldiers reported capturing German soldiers as young as eight years old. Though unskilled, the German children fought with a ferociousness that frightened Allied troops. The Nazis had told their young soldiers that the Allies were monsters who would torture and kill them if they were captured, so many of them fought to the death or committed suicide rather than surrender. Of the five thousand Hitler Youths who fought in the Battle of Berlin at the end of the war, only five hundred survived.

In Adolf Hitler's last public appearance in April of 1945, he emerged from his bunker underneath what was left of the Reich Chancellery building to award the Iron Cross, Nazi Germany's highest honor, to members of the Hitler Youth who had showed bravery on the battlefield. The youngest of them was twelve years old. Hitler committed suicide just ten days later, and within a week Nazi Germany surrendered. But not before it had sacrificed an entire generation of young people to a mad dream of world domination.

After the war, when the Allies had to decide which Nazis to try for war crimes, the Hitler Youth who survived were forgiven because they were children. They had been misguided by their leaders, the Allies decided, who were really to blame. As a part of the "denazification" of Germany, the Allies showed films of the Nazi death camps to German children who had been members of the Hitler Youth and the Bund Deutscher Mädel. Many of them didn't believe the images they saw. They had been so brainwashed by their Nazi leaders that it took years for them to understand that they, and not the Allies, were the monsters. In the years to come, the boys and girls who had been members of the Hitler Youth came to despise Nazi Germany for turning them into soldiers, making them complicit in the Holocaust, and robbing them of their youth.

Projekt 1065 is a work of fiction set against the very real backdrop of Nazi Germany in World War II. Kristallnacht, the Gestapo, the SRD, the concentration camps, the Hitler Youth, the Edelweiss Pirates, the "Aryan" education in German schools—all of that is real. Everything Adolf Hitler says to Michael and the other boys in this book is an actual quote from Hitler; I gathered them together from various speeches and interviews so that I wasn't putting words in Hitler's mouth. Adolf Hitler said enough crazy, awful things that I didn't need to make up anything new for him.

By 1943, the Americans and British were taking turns bombing Berlin, dropping more than 68,000 tons of bombs on the city, and many Allied bomber and fighter pilots had to parachute into enemy territory when their planes were shot out from under them. Some survived and were ferreted to safety by the resistance movement; far more were captured and taken to concentration camps or killed. Nazi children were encouraged to spy on their parents and turn them in for violations, which they often did. The Nazis were great burners of "degenerate" books too, but by 1943, when my story takes place, there weren't many large-scale book burnings anymore—mostly because the Nazis had already rounded up and destroyed all the books they disagreed with.

Ireland *was* officially neutral during World War II, much to the disappointment and disdain of England and the rest of the Allies. The Irish did have an embassy in Berlin during World War II, but Michael and his family are fictional characters. The spying that the O'Shaunessey family does, however, is based in reality. In the 1980s, declassified documents revealed that the Irish diplomatic corps in Europe had been actively collecting intelligence and sending it back to the Allies—at great risk to themselves—throughout World War II. Though her army never fought in the war, Ireland, it turns out, wasn't quite as neutral as everyone had been led to believe.

Real too is Projekt 1065, the actual code name for the secret Nazi project to develop a jet-powered aircraft. In 1944, the Germans succeeded, and the Messerschmitt Me 262 Schwalbe became the world's first operational jet fighter, flying almost a hundred miles an hour faster than any Allied plane in the skies.

By then, it was too little too late, but their invention of the jet engine did change the world. At the end of the war, the Allies snatched up the technology and developed jet planes of their own, and by the 1950s, jet planes began replacing propeller-powered planes in air forces and civilian air travel.

Operation Paperclip, the code name for the real Allied plan to recruit or kidnap Nazi scientists to work for the United States, came a little later than I have used it here, but both the Americans and Russians played a chess game with scientists throughout the war, trying to capture the best brains in Europe for themselves. Both sides were particularly interested in rocket scientists for the coming space race, and in nuclear physicists who could develop an atomic bomb. The Manhattan Project, the code name for the US project that created the world's first nuclear weapon, was a much bigger secret than I have made it here — most people didn't know anything about the development of the atomic bomb until the United States became the first and only nation to use one, dropping atomic bombs on Hiroshima and Nagasaki, Japan, in 1945.

If you're looking to read more about Nazi Germany and the Hitler Youth, I highly recommend Susan Campbell Bartoletti's award-winning book *Hitler Youth: Growing Up in Hitler's Shadow*, which follows twelve different young people growing up in Nazi Germany before and during the war. It was an invaluable resource to me in writing *Projekt 1065*.

ACKNOWLEDGMENTS

Thanks again to my terrific editor Aimee Friedman, to David Levithan, and to everyone behind the scenes at Scholastic: Emily Rader, Joy Simpkins, Nina Goffi, Bess Braswell, Jennifer Abbots, Lizette Serrano, Antonio Gonzalez, Ed Masessa, Jana Haussman, everyone in the Fairs and Clubs, and beyond. You guys are awesome. Special thanks to my fellow Bat Cave writers for their critiques: Renée Ahdieh, Gabrielle Charbonnet, Megan Miranda, Rebecca Petruck, Carrie Ryan, Megan Shepherd, and particularly Gwenda Bond and Terra McVoy. I'd also like to thank my agent Holly Root — welcome to the Gratz Industries team! — and my great friend Bob. I owe a huge debt of gratitude to all the teachers, librarians, and booksellers out there who continue to put my books into the hands of young readers; you know who you are, and you're rock stars! Thank you. And last but never least, much love and thanks to Wendi and Jo.

ABOUT THE AUTHOR

Alan Gratz is the acclaimed author of several books for young readers, including *Prisoner B-3087*, which was named to YALSA's 2014 Best Fiction for Young Adults list; *Code of Honor*, a YALSA 2016 Quick Pick; and *The Brooklyn Nine*, which was among *Booklist*'s Top Ten Sports Books. Alan lives in North Carolina with his wife and daughter. Look for him online at www.alangratz.com.